I0647661

Gaining It At 41
Sarah Butland

All characters and situations in these stories are fictional, and any resemblance to any person, living or dead, is purely coincidental.

Text and illustration 2022 © by Sarah Butland
All rights reserved, including the right to reproduce this book or portions thereof in any form.

First Edition
ISBN 978-0-9937864-8-8

Published by:
Sarah Butland
www.SarahButland.com

Cover designed by Newhook Designs

Sarah Butland books are available at special discounts for bulk purchases for sales promotions, fundraising, or educational use.
Special editions or book excerpts can also be created to specification upon request.

For more information about the author, Sarah Butland, please visit:
http://www.SarahButland.com

For all of those who see light in the darkest of times and realize the chaos will soon be memorable moments.

GAINING IT AT 41

Excerpt from Gaining It At 41

I laughed, nervously, surprised by the question, but then realized it was somewhat justified. I knew I could handle myself, but Chuck was showing a different side to himself that I wasn't used to. "I'm quitting," I blurted out with no thought to the words.

"You are? When did you decide this?" Travis seemed as shocked as I did.

"I guess just now. I want to do more, to work for myself, or stay home or something. I have enough savings for a few months off anyway. Hopefully I can figure out something by then." I sounded a lot more confident than I felt.

"That's amazing! I'm so proud of you. We should celebrate! But first, will you be giving two weeks' notice?"

"I think it's only fair. That gives him some time to replace me or offer me what I'm worth. I don't really know what he could offer, besides his resignation, though. That would convince me to stay, maybe. Travis, why do people dread turning 40? I just did and my life is already so much better for it."

Travis leaned over me then, kissed me with so much passion and determination I felt it in my toenails.

Prologue

188.8 lbs
5'2
BMI – too high
Blood pressure good

8 lbs 3 ounces.

18 inches in length.

A beautiful baby girl that already beat all the odds stacked against her. Brown patches of hair. 10 fingers, 10 toes and yes, blue eyes, but who would know how long those would last.

Abigail Terecia.

There was a reason for that.

Happy birthday to Abigail. Abi for short. I could not believe that at 41 years of age I would be celebrating the birth of my own child. My first, and suspected last, little baby girl being tunneled through my vagina despite experts who recommended this a caesarian section instead of a vaginal birth. Baby had other plans despite the doctor's scheduled delivery date.

My age was a factor. Not to mention my contraceptive measures that failed and delayed menopause that I had to look forward to while raising a toddler. I asked about tying my tubes before the test was positive and they laughed, very unprofessionally, but I had the right. Abigail was a miracle, after all. A healthy miracle child, they told me, after numerous precautions taken not to have her exist at all.

I never knew that this would be my story. I struggled with the last one, but this one, this story of a surprise pregnancy and shocking birth, may be an important for many. I wanted people to know they could get pregnant despite being older, on birth control, and finding their love later in life. I hoped my story of self-discovery and precautions warned many and helped even more.

91% effective they said. 1-2% for a 40 year old without birth control. The chances were small, but I beat them all. The test was positive, the pregnancy was interesting and eventually, Abigail was born.

Having to skip any numbing medications and with the epidural ended up not even being an option, I planned for a c-section, everyone did, it seemed, but apparently Abigail had other plans despite my canal not being quite stretched enough for the doctor's liking.

I wondered what Chuck would say. If he would ask if it was his. Then I remembered, through my stupor, it wouldn't matter. The baby would be Travis's, if he chose to stay. And my time off work was doctor's orders. I had been prescribed the six weeks in the beginning, in hopes of improving the chances of a full term pregnancy. They would need to see me often so it made it easier to be off work to be able to schedule appointments. Then they would determine how much time I'd need. With no benefits it would be hard to take more time. I needed to be stress free. I needed another miracle.

Two miracles actually. I wondered if that was asking too much. The first being that when the doctor tweaked my nipple months ago he assured me I would have no trouble breast feeding and now, with Abigail properly latched, I finally had confidence he was right. That was the one thing my gynecologist seemed right about. The second, simply or not so simply, was a healthy child born at full term.

Even he laughed at me when he confirmed my dozen pregnancy tests were accurate. But I am getting a head of myself, my story doesn't start with Abigail. It starts with Travis so let's go back to that beginning.

With your permission, and to keep you interested, let me rewind about twelve months.

Chapter One

Travis already had everything cancelled for the day as he did every year for his birthday. He explained that while he didn't do much in the way of celebration, he felt having the day off away from the world was something he deserved annually. Thankfully it fell on a day with no classes so he wasn't missing school.

With my birthday behind me and gifting me this gorgeous young man, I knew I needed to do something to make his day special. I just wasn't sure what I could pull off with such short notice. "Penny for your thoughts?"

Clearly, I would never be a good poker player as the look on my face gave my thinking away. I couldn't think with a thousand questions being thrown at me, so I just shrugged and said I needed to get home for a bit. Travis pouted and said he was perfectly content with staying in bed with me, promising that whatever I needed at my place he would provide or could wait.

Thankfully, his sister's timing was perfect as she entered the apartment and called out. "Are you folks decent? I brought bagels." I giggled and it sounded weird to me as I was not a giggler. Travis reached his arms around me and kissed my left shoulder. We were still very much indecent, but I had some planning to do.

I playfully pushed off his advancements and stood on shaky legs, grabbing the clothes I could find from the floor. "Where's my underwear?" I whispered as I saw Travis lean over and grab them.

"Go without today. You don't need these, I do. It is my birthday, after all."

"I thought I was your present?" The thought of going without panties sent shivers through me, mainly through my previously numb clitoris, so I agreed. Very inexperienced at this flirting thing, I tried to dress as seductively as I could as he ogled me and yelled to Kate that we just needed a few minutes.

Once I was almost fully dressed, noting how bare my vagina felt, I took in the scene of Travis finding his clothes and, making a production of putting on pants without underwear, too. He was a boxers, not briefs guy, which delighted me though I wasn't really sure why. I felt my vagina discrete liquid that warmed the inside of my leg and giggled again, delighted that I wasn't yet old enough to deal with uncomfortable dryness. Travis approached me, put his hand on my crotch and rubbed slightly before opening the door and taking my hand as we left his bedroom.

"How did the interview go, sis?" Travis recovered much more quickly than I ever could. I'm sure she could tell I was still frazzled by the colour of my cheeks. I just hoped she couldn't smell the sex coming off me, or out of the room.

A dozen New York Style bagels sat in an open box and six hot drinks beside them, still steaming. "I had no idea what you drank so I got one of everything. You choose first."

"I think Travis should go first, it is his birthday after all."

"Oh right, big bro. Your birthday indeed. An exciting day for all of us it seems. You pick first but leave the best for your girl. Am I right in assuming that's what this is?"

Travis, still holding my hand, leaned over to kiss me on the cheek to seal the deal. "I guess it is, right Annabelle?"

"Damn right!" I laughed and grabbed a bagel. "I'm starving and need to run. Thanks for these. How was the interview?" I started getting my shoes and jacket on as we chatted.

"They are calling me back with an offer later today! It's not my dream job but it certainly could lead to that. Especially with this little one coming, I need something flexible but with the potential of long term." Kate instinctively rubbed her belly as she mentioned her little one.

"That's great!" I said between chews and hugged her. "Travis, I need you to pick your drink so I can grab mine and run. I'll be back though."

"Ok, Boss Lady. I'm all about the black coffee and think that you would like this one," he scanned them over, chose one and handed to me. "Butterscotch Mocha Supreme, sweet and caffeinated."

"That does sound delicious, as is this bagel. You know me so well already! Ok, I'll be back in an hour." The birthday day ideas were already forming with my first sip of delicious mocha, but I needed to hurry. "Congratulations again, Kate and I'll see you soon, Travis."

"I'll miss you in the meantime," he said and kissed my nose as I turned to go.

"Ooo la la," I heard his sister comment as the door closed behind me. I couldn't help but giggle again.

I felt terrible lying to Travis, but I wasn't going home and I didn't need to be anywhere. I was surprised, however, that he didn't offer to drive me, but was also thankful he didn't as I would hate to continue the lie. I needed to walk to clear my head and prayed silently that Megan was working as I entered the store. I scanned the cash registers, but she wasn't there, so I asked one of them if she was in.

"She just went on break actually, she should be close. Do you need me to page her? Or is it something I can help you with?"

I hesitated, not wanting to cause her alarm or bother her at work, but figured she would want an update. "Yes, please page her, thank you," I heard myself say. The young man called her over the intercom. I stood to the side, letting the customers through and waited. I saw her coming down the aisle in a rush and walked quickly towards her. "It's ok, everything is fine. It's just me. Sorry for bothering you."

Her face lit up as she embraced me and shuffled me through an 'employees only' door tucked in behind the pharmacy. "Are you sure this is ok?"

"Oh, what are they going to do, tell my boss? Now spill! How did it go, tell me everything… well, no, not everything, but let me live through your new romance."

"Slow down, Megan. I will, I promise, but not now. I only have a minute, as I suspect you do, too. I just need some ideas. It's Travis's birthday and I want to do something to surprise him."

She looked me up and down and grinned, "I think spending the night with him after all that drama was gift enough, no?" She winked for emphasis, like I had only seen in movies before. It made me grin wider and almost hop with glee. I realized how grateful I was for her friendship. She was giving me confidence and restoring my faith in lasting relationships.

"Yes, yes, I spent the night and it was fabulous and I'll fill you in on everything later, but I need a plan for today."

"Here's what you do…" and she quietly told me the most brilliant plan that would actually work on short notice.

Chapter Two

I took an Uber from the store to home for a quick shower and dressed in new lingerie, putting comfortable, but still flattering, clothes on top. I made a quick call to Fabio's to make a reservation and then grabbed an Uber back to Travis'.

On the short ride I haphazardly wrapped a little something I found at the store that would lead the way of a day filled with riddles, rhymes and romance. It all come together so quickly it felt like magic and I never really believed in that stuff. My life was starting to change in a fantastic way and I was all for it.

Once wrapped, I texted Travis to be ready and to meet me outside. We would take the same Uber, Frank was the drivers name and, if I wasn't already smitten, I would have thought he was a handsome gentleman, and drive until Travis solved the first clue. Frank was fully supportive of my plans and said he wanted a day of fun anyway, so he was our designated driver.

We only waited a couple of minutes for Travis to appear. While waiting, and assuming it was safe, I texted Kate starting with – DO NOT SAY IT'S ME. Followed by a second text of MEET ME AT PINE'S DELI AT 1 PM IF YOU CAN. BDAY

SURPRISE. Once sent, Travis appeared fully dressed and showered, though I had to wonder if he left his boxers at home. He got into the back of the car with me, a puzzled look on this face, leaned over to kiss me and buckled up. I handed him his gift.

"Didn't I tell you that you were gift enough?"

"If you did, I didn't understand what that meant. Open it. Frank here won't drive until you do." I winked at the driver then laughed. I never giggled and I never, ever winked, but here I was breaking all of my rules in the same day. Travis's birthday must be a special day, now to make it a memorable one.

While Travis opened his gift I heard my phone's text notification sound but had to ignore it. I figured it was Kate and she could wait. As he pulled back the wrapping and revealed a box of condoms, the seal already broken which was my own doing, but foreshadowed so much. Frank looked away, seemingly curious but trying to be polite. Travis looked shocked as he looked first to Frank then to me.

"Remember, it was the ones you were looking at when we met at the store?"

"Oh yes, I just, why are you gifting me this in a car? With a spectator?" His free hand found its way to my inner thigh and he squeezed. Frank still didn't drive away and seemed to be so patient.

"Not here. I'll put them in my bag after you solve the riddle. Look inside." He pulled his hand from my thigh, slowly and seemingly reluctantly, and I immediately felt a chill. Eager for his hand to return, I watched as he pulled the slip of paper from the box.

It took him a second and then his eyes got wide, he put the paper back in the box and handed it to me asking the driver, "To the college please. I have a crime to solve!" As I giggled and put the box in my bag I secretly wished for Travis to return his hand to my thigh. My wish was his command, of course, as he went a little further in and rubbed his pinky against my sensitive spot, all while carrying on a conversation with Frank. Things were heating up quickly and it wasn't even 11 AM yet.

My breathing became heavier as we drove the fifteen minutes to the college and Travis continued his conversation and rubbing. Trying to focus on the tasks at hand I struggled to think of how to place the next clue without being obvious and giving its location away. Harder, still, as I only passed by the school a couple of times and never with the intention of returning to hide something. Near impossible to think with my temperature rising while Travis rubbed all the right spots and my trying to enjoy it while holding back groans and the need to reciprocate.

Privy to some of the plan, when Frank got out of the car and opened my door he grabbed the clue discretely while inviting us to stay in the car. "I'm just going to see if there are security guards or students in the park. I'm not technically parked legally, but this was the closest I could get to where Ms Annabelle wanted to be." He finished with a wink as I whispered a thank you and he was off. This bit would be a surprise even to me.

As soon as my door was closed, Travis leaned over to disconnect my seatbelt, his was already undone apparently, and he awkwardly leaned into embrace my neck with his mouth. I groaned in response, confident this would leave a mark but truly not caring. I was learning many things, including how naughty it was to feel a penis become erect. The windows started steaming up and I completely lost track of time and space while I closed my eyes and enjoyed the feelings. A knock on the window startled me and I pushed Travis away.

Opening the door I apologized to Frank as Travis followed me out on the same side.

"Everything is in place, Ms Annabelle." He seemed unfazed and I wondered how many drunk young couples he saw making out in the back of his car. Only I wasn't young or drunk, but I do believe I was quickly falling in love. And it wasn't with Frank. Though he was quickly becoming a friend.

Frank got back in the car, clue free, as we wandered to the campus grounds and I knew immediately where the clue was hidden. A statue stood of a former mayor and, thankfully weather was on my side, I caught sight of the folded paper tucked in the man's fist.

Travis took my hand and led me straight to it but, before reading it, leaned me against the back of the statue and went back to kissing a spot on my neck. I leaned back, closed my eyes and embraced the delightful feeling for a moment. Groaning in ecstasy I felt embarrassed and, once again, gently pushed him back. "Not here but please, somewhere again soon," my breath was lost in the wind.

"It's my birthday, though. Don't I have a say?" I took the clue out of his hand and showed it to him.

"Not yet," I answered. "For now, your fans await."

Chapter Three

This clue took him a bit longer to solve and I loved the suspense. "Any hints?"

"Nah… you'll get it. I have faith."

He sat on the edge of the statues base, I sat beside him and timidly laid my hand on his inner thigh, repaying him for earlier. He laid a hand on mine as he looked away to nothing in particular. I moved my hand closer to his penis and wondered again about his boxers. He squeezed my hand just as I got to the tip. "By golly, I think I know! Let's go."

Getting into the car he told Frank, "To Pine's Deli please, Frank." Travis turned his head to me and, after I nodded in confirmation, buckled up and we were on our way. I picked up my phone to as we rode to ensure everything was in place. We were earlier than I expected, but it would have to do. I groaned when I saw the first message was from Chuck.

"Are you not coming in today?" the text stated.

I clearly remembered him telling me to take the day off after our trip, delighted that it worked out so well not only with it being Travis's birthday, but also because I needed some time to consider my job options. The trip, for work, was much more than I bargained for. It was a sneak peek into a relationship with Chuck outside of the office and a delightful reprieve when Travis showed up. That trip solidified I no longer wanted to work for Chuck, no matter how comfy of a job it was or how much they paid me. I couldn't work with someone so cruel and finally understood that I deserved better. "What's wrong, Annabelle?"

"It's Chuck. He expected me to come to work today after telling me, insisting, I take the day off and just go back on Monday. I don't know what to do with that guy."

Travis looked upset, clearly confused by the way his eye brows arched and lips bent. I was impressed with how quickly I was picking up on his nuances. "No, I mean, job wise. I'm done with him, clearly. Juggling multiple men was too much and you won my heart, hands down. It's the working for a jerk of a boss I don't want to do anymore, but can't afford to be unemployed."

It startled me when Frank replied, "Drive Uber, like me. Good people, quick pay and work when you want to." He said it with a laugh and I nervously and automatically responded with a chuckle, but deep down something sparked. Not yet a flame or even bringing warmth, but an idea that would nag me for weeks.

"Thanks, Frank. I'll look into that. I think I'm almost qualified for it, I think I would just need a license, right?" It was my turn to laugh, only this time it was tinged with embarrassment. I hadn't told Travis that I never drove before, only that I didn't own a car as transportation in the city was so convenient. Turning to him, I noticed he wasn't paying much attention to the conversation anymore and, instead, was staring out the window.

"Travis? My turn to ask –everything ok?"

He came out of his stupor and replied, "Yes, yes, sorry, I was just thinking about my mother and her fondness of birthdays. She always spoiled us so completely it's just sad she can't anymore. You would have loved her, she would have loved you and completely approved of this adventure."

"That's sweet of you to say. I'm so sorry she isn't here with us anymore but I hope that I make her proud every day. And I know you do. You're such a loving person. You never did tell me her name."

"Terecia. It was her grandmother's name, too. She went by her middle name, though. Lucy."

"That's beautiful. I'd like to know more. Why did she go by her middle name?"

Frank pulled up to the deli just as it started to rain. We didn't have time to chat about his mother's name, so my curiousity would remain. Travis opened his door while I just sat for an extra second. "You go in, Travis. I need to reply to Chuck." It was a little white lie as I had already replied to him, I needed a beat to let Kate know we were coming in. 'All set?' I wrote and hit send then waited. Travis closed the door and hurried to the overhang of the deli, being a gentleman and not going in yet while also not hovering as I wrote my text.

"Frank, I think we're ok from here. I don't know how long dinner will be and I don't want to keep you."

"It has been a blast. I wish you luck with your job endeavours and love adventures, Ms Annabelle. I hope I find a love as sweet as yours someday. And if you want to chat about being an Uber driver, after your license test I mean, let me know." He handed me a card with his direct number on it.

"I'm sure you will find someone to love. I didn't think I would and here I am, and you're much younger than me," I said and I meant it. I couldn't believe how different my life became so quickly. I was always the jealous one, never the one making people jealous. I handed him a bundle of cash as my phone beeped. Thankfully, it was from Kate confirming all was in place. As I got out of the car and onto the sidewalk I said a prayer that I wouldn't hear from Chuck again until Monday. Praying was not something I was used to doing either, though it seemed appropriate in the moment. This was going to be a fantastic weekend of grand adventures, I didn't need him continuing to weigh me down. Which also left a bad feeling deep down in my heart as he was the man to take my virginity, he would always mean something more to me than a jerk boss.

I hustled under the overhang and then saw Travis had opened the door for me at just the perfect time. I didn't even pause as I hurried in and felt him follow right behind me.

"Surprise!" the crowd yelled. Not a great crowd, being lunch time on a work day, but Kate did ok and even Megan was there. Most of the people I didn't recognize at all but trusted that I would get to know them. I knew Kate would know more of his friends then me, even being new to the area.

Travis gave me a quick kiss before leading the way to a man, or rather a teenager. Looking around I noticed that most must have been classmates as they were just babies. And then I laughed. I guess Travis was closer to their age than my own, but seemed so mature compared to them. "This is Mitchell, he's my partner for most of the projects. Mitchell, this is my other partncr. The projects I do with her are much more… intense."

We all laughed, awkwardly, and I wasn't sure if shaking hands was the right thing to do in this situation, a hug or … well, apparently fist bumps were proper. I did a lot of fist bumping and name swapping for the next fifteen minutes and then a table in the back was filled with sandwiches and desserts. It was haphazard but would suffice and was marvelous for such short notice.

The deli wasn't very big but we were able to mingle and people came and went, grabbing a few bites and some words between them. Time passed quickly and Travis seemed so delighted by it all. He somehow seemed especially proud of me as I paraded me around and ensured he introduced me to everyone, even his professor, which was the most awkward. "Joey?" I recognized him before he did me. "Professor Chisholm, meet…" Travis blurted before realizing I already called his professor by his first name.

"Annabelle? What are you doing here? How do you know Travis?" Joey looked from me to Travis and saw that we were holding hands. I was quickly embarrassed and let go, shoving my hand into my pocket.

"Travis is, well…" It was hard for me to get out, to explain and label what Travis was to me. Joey Chisholm was my babysitter decades before. Just eight years my senior, he was the coolest sitter I ever had. So cool I absolutely adored and crushed on him. He lived just next door and looked after me at least weekly until I was twelve. Sometimes even after that if my parents were away overnight. What a strange world.

"We're dating," Travis declared. "It's new but it's wonderful."

"Yes, yes, we're going out now. I didn't know you were his professor! It's been so long. Are you still with Angela?"

"I can't believe you remembered her name! We split years ago, have two kids together, one is actually named after you. We call her Annie, and then there is Thomas, our oldest. My gosh, it's been a long time. Little Annabelle. The easiest girl on the block."

Travis choked on the drink at his words. "Excuse me?"

I was seeing jealousy rear its head for the second time that day and it took me a second to realize how he heard what Joey said. Joey laughed, catching on faster, and apologized. "Easiest girl to babysit. Travis, I babysat her. She was eight ye-, ahem, Eight Filly Lane, I was Six. Easy to walk to, walk home from and most behaved for me to get paid to watch." I was horrified that he was going to say I was eight years younger than him. Clearly he saw that the difference in age between Travis and I was much greater. Was I under thinking the age gap or over thinking my feelings? Only time would tell and, ironically, timing was everything these days.

Chapter Four

It was only Kate, Travis, Megan and I left, along with the employees, two hours later. Megan and I offered to help clean up, but our assistance was refused. The deli owners were delighted to have such a large, and mostly new, crowd in on an otherwise typically slow day of the week. Many of the party attendees even promised to return which was wonderful.

Kate mentioned she had paid the bill already and refused to accept my reimbursement, saying with all the excitement she forgot about Travis' birthday and he would kill her if he knew. She told us to move onto the other part of our day and she would finish up with the deli.

Travis was sitting in the corner with the third clue, puzzled and stuffed from the delicious meal of ham and cheese sandwiches and Nanaimo bars. We had time so I let him ponder and stood back to watch him quietly.

"Rascal's!" It wasn't 5 p.m. yet but Jack rushed from the party to get things ready at the bar early. We walked there, though our legs were jelly from all the standing and mingling at the party. It was nice to hold hands, be in public and enjoy the fresh air. It would be an early night for us both and I was definitely looking forward to it, not having much sleep all week.

Before going into the bar through the back door in the alley, Travis leaned me against the bricks and kissed me. Hard. My body reacted quickly, all my erogenous parts tingling and I kissed him back. Running my tongue against his teeth, swirling it around and taking in the taste of ham and coconut. The mix of tastes should have been unpleasant, but was delightful and made the moment even more memorable. And then Joey's face came to mind.

I must have froze, just slightly, as Travis pulled back and asked, out of breath, if something was wrong.

"God no!" I felt guilty but still tingled greatly from his touch. "Shall we go in?"

Travis took another second to look in my eyes and then reached out to open the door, "After you." He pinched my ass as I walked in front of him, slowly to allow my eyes to adjust to the candle light. I held Travis's hand and led him to the bar, the side he was rarely on, and we both sat on stools. A candle stood lit in the middle of two red headed sluts; the drink, not actual people. He laughed, his gorgeous tender laugh, and picked up his glass. "Shall I make a toast?"

"If you'd like to have the honours." I picked up mine and waited.

"To birthdays - the happiest days ever."
"Cheers." We clinked our glasses and then our lips met again. He almost fell from his stool as he leaned so far over, but I balanced him as I kissed back.

"Shall we take this upstairs?" He whispered as he moved his mouth to my earlobe and sucked slightly. "I didn't see another clue."

Jack's instructions were to leave after lighting the candles and pouring the drinks. I hoped at that moment he was long gone and locked the doors. We didn't have much time before the bar would be opened to the public.

"You didn't look hard enough then." I whispered back as I reluctantly stood and motioned for him to follow. As I did I began to undress, pulling my shirt over my head and leaving it behind. The clue was in the bra of my lingerie. He couldn't see it yet with my back to him as I began to unzip the back of my pants. I looked back over my shoulder to see him hurrying behind me and he grabbed my breasts from behind.

As he did he felt the paper, grabbing it as he turned me around to kiss me. "It's too late to play hard to get. Why are you making me chase you?"

Even in the shadows of the candle light I could see his throbbing penis through his jeans and shivered with excitement. This clue was the easiest of all as I knew I couldn't restrain myself for long. It simply said – rack me up.

On the way to the pool table he took off his shirt, kicked off his shoes and fumbled with his jeans. I noticed with pure ecstasy that he didn't bother with boxers. I laid on the pool table and he won the game with his stick. Between us, we only needed one stick for this game and the cues were obvious. No chalk needed. And we both won. A few times.

Chilled after our escapades, and knowing we needed to clean up before opening, I quickly dressed despite my weak and wobbly knees. I didn't waste time with undergarments, and encouraged Travis to go upstairs.

"It's your birthday, you shouldn't have to clean."

"But you can barely walk and have done a lot of work today to prepare. And, we've had a lot of play so I don't mind balancing the scales. Working together will speed up the pace, and, not to mention, I'd be lonely without you."

"Sounds fair," I said through chattering teeth as I struggled into my clothes. "Can you get a crate for the candles and I'll start blowing them out."

Through a series of giggles Travis noted, "You are damn good at blowing things." I pushed him away and told him to go get a crate.

We cleaned up in record time and scurried up the stairs as Jack took his place at the bar and unlocked the front door.

Chapter Five

With the festivities over and the clues all solved, I almost felt relieved to see Kate at the stove preparing dinner. "I figured you two would need refueling after the day you had so I'm here just to make dinner and then leave. I rented a movie for you to watch and will be out of your hair for a few hours. I tried to find a place to spend the night but no one came through for me so I will be back to sleep. I can get ear plugs, though." She ended her speech with a wink that somehow seemed knowing and didn't embarrass me.

"Thanks, Sis. For all you did today. This was the best birthday in a long time, maybe ever. What movie?"

"Gremlins, of course."

"Oh, I never saw that one," I commented. "Is it good?"

Travis and Kate both gasped and looked shocked and disappointed. "You haven't?" Travis exclaimed. It was a classic yet still not on Netflix or even Amazon Prime so had to be rented.

"Where have you been these last…?" Kate asked but decided not to finish.

"I guess not watching the right movies. Why don't you stay though, Kate? Really, I don't think Travis would mind either, would you?"

"Gremlins is a classic Kate and I watched at least once a year. Usually on her birthday as it's closer to Christmas but, it's time for new traditions. Please do stay, Kate. We need to celebrate your job, too and I can't be the only one sharing this memorable night with Annabelle. Besides," he said as he stirred the pot of spaghetti, "you made enough to feed a small army."

"I've never been good at measuring pasta and it does smell delicious, if I do say so myself. If you don't think I'm imposing, of course I'll stay." Kate set out three plates and a bottle of white wine, adding a glass to the two sitting on the counter. "Thanks, guys."

We ate a delicious meal, complete with garlic bread, and Travis and I took the couch while Kate sat in the single recliner. We invited her to join us on the comfortable couch, arguing it was plenty big, but she refused, covering us up with a blanket as we laid into each other and finding a blanket of her own before taking the chair.

Kate started the movie and then realized she left the popcorn in the microwave and told us not to bother pausing the movie. Travis did anyway and while she went into the kitchen to retrieve the popcorn and a new bottle of wine, Travis' hands discreetly found their way under my shirt and to my nipples. Exhausted from the day's events, the touch had a more tickling effect than sexual and I let out yet another giggle. "Just making sure they are still there," Travis whispered as he moved his hand to on top of the blanket before Kate returned.

"I did wonder if you were going to bite them clean off earlier," I whispered and punctuated it with a kiss.

Although I enjoyed the movie, the day's events and lack of sleep all week did me in and I was asleep in no time. Being cozy and warm, with the steady beat of Travis's heart, and after a few glasses of wine, I was content and at peace. I woke once, ready to apologize, only to realize Travis was sound asleep too, the room was dark, television off and Kate was missing.

Drifting off easily again I slept the night through and woke to hear the door close and be locked. Sitting up I looked to Travis who appeared to wake recently, too. "Good morning, Gremlin," he said softly and with a smile. "You liked the movie, huh?"

"I liked what I saw but I'm loving what I see now more. What are your plans today?"

"I have none, you?"

"Why don't we grab some breakfast and watch the movie now, if you don't think Kate would mind. Where was she off to this early?"

Checking his watch Travis reported, "It's 11:08 a.m. Not early at all. She must be going to buy some work clothes. And she wouldn't mind at all. I think that's a grand plan." He got up and went to the kitchen, searching the cupboards. "Oatmeal or Cornflakes? There may also be some bagels left."

"Blueberries?" He looked into the freezer and was happy to report they had a bag of blueberries. "Oatmeal then?"

"Sounds wonderful. Maybe a bagel while I wait?" I agreed, and was starving. He toasted the bagel and added a bit of butter then delivered with a kiss, morning breath and all. Both were delicious.
He returned to the kitchen to make the oatmeal, adding the blueberries while the oatmeal cooked along with a touch of brown sugar. I was smitten to see he was making it on the stove and not using the microwave. Scooping it into two bowls he returned to the couch, handing me one of them. We struggled to wrap the blankets around us, with one hand each and he started the movie. I stayed awake the entire time, filled my belly with oatmeal and then we escaped to the shower together, hoping Kate would be out for a bit longer.

Once out I realized I didn't have a change of clothes and should give Travis his space, at least for a few hours, so mentioned I thought it was time to get home.

"How about I go with you?"

"You're serious? Don't you want some time alone to study or something?"

"It feels like this is our honeymoon and I don't want to spend a second apart. But if you do, I won't be offended. I figured we should maybe sleep separate tomorrow tonight as you'll have work and I have school but I'm not ready quite yet. I also have to work tonight, remember? Real world stuff."

He was sweet, and right, so I invited him back to my place. We called an Uber, still physically exhausted even with the good night's sleep, and Frank picked us up. Remembering us, he asked about the day and Travis excitedly spilled most of the details. It made me feel the proudest I ever felt, hearing him brag me up and tell an almost stranger how much fun he had. As he chatted I squeezed his thigh and he took a break from speaking to give me a peck on the cheek.

The car ride home passed quickly and we said our goodbyes to Frank, sluggishly making it up to my apartment where I invited Travis into the shower. Hearing him talk about the day made me horny despite my lack of energy. He was more than ready to accept my invitation.

We spent the rest of the day being lazy and mixing our time with naps and talking about our pasts and futures. I admired how sure Travis was of his next five years as I could only guess at where mine would take me.

Chapter Six

Travis had to work Saturday night so we went our separate ways after supper. I invited him to come back for the night but he refused, saying he was working the late shift and wouldn't want to wake me but would see me Sunday.

I was dreading Sunday as it was the day before Monday and a full work week with Chuck, so was eager for the distraction. When Travis left around 5 p.m. to get ready for his shift, I tidied up, plugged in my powerless phone and made my way to the bath with a book.

Reading and soaking for an hour, I was relaxed enough to just crawl into bed where I read another chapter. I was kind of surprised Travis didn't call on his break, but drifted off to sleep before realizing I didn't turn my phone back on.

Not waking until the next morning, I finally felt rested and was so absorbed in the book I picked it up before making breakfast. I had to go back a chapter and a half to make sense as to what I read before long blinks the night before took over and then suddenly realized my phone was off.

I put the book on the bed, got up and ran to the living room where I plugged it in. Releasing it from its cord, I held the power button and willed it to turn on faster. When it finally did, the notifications poured in. Looking down at my home screen I saw that twenty-seven new text messages were waiting for me and gasped. I didn't think they would all be from Travis, as he knew I was exhausted and that I wasn't going anywhere, but then I worried who else they would be from

There was only one way to find out.

I entered my password and opened the messages app. The most recent one was from Travis so it showed on top. I put my finger on it to open and saw only three were from him. A thank you and miss you in one, and I love you in the third with a wish that I was sleeping well and the third was to call me when I got up, no matter how early. Each touching and heartfelt in its own way. Not too aggressive, instead showing understanding and sweet affection. I re-read them before first taking a breath and opening the next most recent chain.

Mike.

Seventeen messages from Mike.

Each more aggressive than the last, which convinced me that I would need to change my number as well as address in the near future. I didn't want to move at all, didn't want to change my habits or bother with the hassle, but I hated that he knew where I lived. I started to scold myself for being so stupid, so smitten, to fall so easily for a jerk like that but stopped. He had his good side and was able to schmooze me out of my shell. Without him I don't know if I would have been brave enough to keep up with Travis.

Deleting all the messages and adding Mike's number to my blocked caller list, I was impressed it was so easy to do my first time around. Maybe Travis's younger ways were rubbing off on me without even knowing it.

That done, I looked to the next set of messages.

Chuck.

The first was about work, reminding me that I did need to go into the office on Monday, giving me the impression he still conveniently forgot he told me not to go in on Friday. The last two got personal. One was a picture I would have rather not have seen, and the last reminding me to be professional at the office. That our relationship was not to be discussed at the office.

"Well, duh!" I exclaimed. Much easier to do now that there really wasn't a relationship at all. He needed to move on and get over himself.

I called Travis and, though I could tell I woke him, he denied it. "Sorry, you said…"

"I know. I wanted to see you as soon as I could. Did you have a good sleep?"

"I did. I can't believe how long I slept, but am feeling refreshed again. Thank you for not being annoyed when I didn't answer your texts. I had a bath when you left and then fell asleep."

"Of course. I figured you would be exhausted after your trip and meetings, not to mention all the activities that followed. I sense something is wrong though, what's up?"

I loved and hated how he could hear my feelings through my voice already. As much as I tried to hide that the other texts didn't bother me, deep down they were irritating. I hesitated with telling him, making a bigger deal out of it than should be made but did need someone to confide in.

"Mike and Chuck both text me incessantly." As if on cue, another notification sounded and I looked at my phone briefly. "Are still texting me. I figured out how to block Mike's number but can't really do that with Chuck. I just... I don't know what I ever saw in either of those jerks."

"Don't blame yourself, Annabelle. You were experimenting, finding out what you really liked and I am pleased as punch that you landed on me. I'm coming over, we'll figure out a plan." I didn't usually love when people invited themselves over, I mean, I guess it never really happened to me before but I was eager to see his face. We hung up our respective phones and I got in the shower, eager to see what he'd bring for breakfast as he promised. I really needed to do a grocery run and prepare meals for the week, but it would wait.

Travis arrived with breakfast sandwiches from Pine's that were amazing. We ate together at the table, talking and laughing before getting into more serious topics. Hesitant to make much out of the texts, I let Travis introduce the topic and he did so once we retired to the couch. "Let's tackle Mike first. He's a nuisance and I'm glad you figured out how to block him. If somehow something more happens, he starts showing up at your door, call me immediately. We'll figure something out. Hopefully he'll lose interest once he realizes you're not wasting your time with him."

"I hate it though, what if he just needs a sponsor? Would I even qualify? I do feel responsible in a complicated way. And guilty. I was the cause of his relapse."

"Don't," Travis took both my hands in his. "This is not your fault. You had no idea how weak he was and, if it was anything like our beginning, you were clear on your expectations. This is all Mike. He has a problem and should find his own solution. Agreed?"

"Yeah, I guess so. I just…"

"No. Stop. He has issues that go far beyond being single and he needs to realize that. You have done what you can for him and now it's up to him."

"You're right, just give me time."

"You can have all the time you need, well, maybe just a week as I want you all to myself. But then there's Chuck who really isn't going anywhere so you need to figure out where you want to go. Do you feel safe going back to the office tomorrow?"

I laughed, nervously, surprised by the question, but then realized it was somewhat justified. I knew I could handle myself, but Chuck was showing a different side to himself that I wasn't used to. "I'm quitting," I blurted out with no thought to the words.

"You are? When did you decide this?" Travis seemed as shocked as I did.

"I guess just now. I want to do more, to work for myself, or stay home or something. I have enough savings for a few months off anyway. Hopefully I can figure out something by then." I sounded a lot more confident than I felt.

"That's amazing! I'm so proud of you. We should celebrate! But first, will you be giving two weeks' notice?"

"I think it's only fair. That gives him some time to replace me or offer me what I'm worth. I don't really know what he could offer, besides his resignation, though. That would convince me to stay, maybe. Travis, why do people dread turning 40? I just did and my life is already so much better for it."

Travis leaned over me then, kissed me with so much passion and determination I felt it in my toenails. When he let me up for air I stopped him from going further with the statement, "I need to go get groceries." Travis sat back again and laughed before saying he'd go with me.

Chapter Seven

Travis and I got groceries together which was a lot of fun. Travis raced down the aisles on the cart, we played hide and seek as we gathered what we wanted each other to try and the time flew by quickly. He offered to take me out to dinner after we put the groceries away, neither of us feeling much like cooking, but I negotiated. We ordered in while he and I prepared lunches, for both of us, for the week. We made an adventure of that, too and had a bit of dessert before supper arrived.

When the intercom sounded, Travis quickly pulled on his pants and went down to grab it, saving me from having to get dressed and cleaned up from the whipped cream. Like promised, I stayed right where I was despite the chill. I was startled when I heard the knock at my door and then realized the door locked when it closed behind him and he didn't have a key.

Finding some courage I ran to the door, without getting dressed, and opened it wide then shut it quickly, or tried to. Mike's hand reached in to ensure the door didn't slam on his face and stopped me. "You're apologizing, I see. I accept." He took a few steps toward me as I backed up and searched for my robe. He closed the door behind him but, once again, it didn't close. Travis stopped it this time.

"Get out!" he yelled. "Get the hell out!"

"Oh, who's this? Your hired stripper? Oh wait, he's not old enough to do much more than dog walking professionally."

As I tripped backwards over my robe and onto the couch, I saw Travis drop the bag of food and, with the same hand, hit Mike square in the jaw. I scrambled to get my robe as I screamed for Mike to leave. Mike stumbled toward Travis who then quickly opened the door and booted him out, quickly closing and locking it while telling me to call the police.

I hesitated, it was over and Mike was gone, but Travis was insistent. I would need to move, no doubt about it, but I would wait until I had a restraining order filed. Just like that, I had no guilt over dumping Mike and I was completely giddy over the display of masculinity Travis presented. As I talked to the 911 operator I went to the freezer and found the new bag of peas we bought, holding them gingerly to Travis's knuckles. Once I was able to disconnect the call, with assurances the police were on their way, I kissed each of his knuckles gently and then his lips softly. "Thank you and I'm sorry."

"Annabelle, that wasn't your fault. I wish you would start having more confidence to know when people are just jerks and not feel the blame."

"Who is the younger one here, Travis? Such wisdom, and I know it's true, but it's not so easy to shift my mindset."

"You didn't think switching to being romantic and wooed would be an easy task either," he winked. I noticed him flinch when I absent mindedly went to grab his hand. "Does it hurt?"

"Only when someone is squeezing it," he teased. "I guess we'll need to get dressed before the police show up. And wait for supper, huh?" He grabbed the bag of supper with his left hand and put it in a clearing on the counter. I found my clothes and dressed then helped Travis into his shirt just in time for another knock at the door. I startled, noticeably, and Travis hugged me from behind, awkwardly, as I peered through the door hole. Confirming it was an officer, I opened the door and let him in.

Travis and I recounted the story, with me providing a little more context and sympathy. The officer made notes and then asked if I would like to press charges. Turning to Travis he must have recognized my hesitation as he answered,

"Annabelle, if you don't I will. I was part of this, too." While I wondered if he was right, as he was actually the one who punched Mike and not the other way around, I decided it didn't matter.

"Will he go to jail?"

"Once my partner finds him, he's searching the building now, he'll be in lock up until his court appearance. Then it's up to the courts."

Thinking he could sober up with a few nights in lock up, I agreed to press charges. The officer's radio sounded and I heard a man report that they found someone matching the description I gave, but to bring down the victim to confirm. "Well, what did

I tell you? Officer Brayson doesn't give up. Can you come down to the car identify him?"

I looked to Travis who nodded and took my hand.

"He'll be in handcuffs, right?" I was more concerned with retaliation against Travis than for myself.

"Better yet, in handcuffs and in the back of the car. Nothing will happen to either of you, we promise."

We made our way out of the building to confirm it was Mike they had in custody. I breathed a sigh of relief and was pretty sure I heard Travis do the same.

When the car pulled way I could see Mike turn and glare at us both but I just smiled, finally finding a bit of that confidence Travis alluded to.

"Supper then dessert?" I asked.

"Did you sneak in some unhealthy treat without telling me?"

"No, no, nothing like that. What I have in mind will be good for your waistline, trust me." I winked as I led the way back up the stairs, holding his left hand as I went.

We had dessert first.

Chapter Eight

Returning to work was awkward but, on the way in, I asked Betty, our secretary, to schedule a fifteen minute meeting as soon as possible for Charles and me. "He's free now if you want to just go in. Actually, he said he wanted to see you right away so now is the perfect time."

Perfect for whom, I thought?

Taking a deep breath after dropping my things off in my office, even before logging into the computer, I made my way across the hall to Chuck's office and knocked on the door. Quickly, before he answered, I stood in the superman pose I heard so much about and did feel a bit better. At least I wouldn't have to dread this meeting, I could just get it over with quickly.

When I was invited in I was startled to see balloons, flowers and every staff member smiling back at me. "Congratulations!" they exclaimed as I timidly walked towards the desk with cake on it. So much for the superman pose, I mumbled on my way.

Chuck stood from behind his desk and explained. "We landed a big client. No wait, let me go back. You landed our biggest client just a few weeks into the job! It's very impressive and deserves to be celebrated. I know it's early but, please, help yourself to some cake."

Looking down at the cake I was surprised to see that it had a picture of Chuck and me from the conference. I didn't even recall it being taken, but thank goodness it wasn't more touchy-feely than it was. If anyone was already onto us they would think the closeness of the subjects were a little more personal than professional.

I sensed eager co-workers behind me, all there just for the cake, so I took a piece and stepped out of the way. The cake was delicious, there was no denying that, and even though it was early I went in for a second piece promising myself to return to the gym the next day.

When the office was cleared out and it was only Chuck and I left, I thanked him again for the celebration and congratulated him for the big win for his company. "I couldn't have done it without you. Which is confirmable truth as we never did it and now look at us. Our company will be set now for the next recession."

"Don't jinx it."

"I couldn't, not with you at the front of things. People love you, I love you." The last bit was more personal than professional by his tone which only served to remind me what I actually came to his office for.

"About that, Charles. I'm afraid I'm not going to be at the front of things much longer. I'm giving you my resignation. I'll help you hire my replacement or make some recommendations but, I need to go out on my own. Your encouragement and belief in me only helped convince me that I was ready."

"You're a bitch! How can you do this now?" He escalated much faster than I thought, but instead of cowering I bit back.

"I don't need to stay two weeks. I was going to do that out of respect, but if there's no mutual respect back I'll leave now."

"Sorry, my fault. I haven't been getting much sleep lately with my move and everything. I actually lucked out and got an apartment in your building so we could more easily discuss business, of course. I'm surprised you didn't see me moving in. 2B. Just below you, actually."

"Chuck. You've gone too far. I'm out of here and I'll be moving, too."

With Mike knowing where I lived and invading my space, and now Chuck being in the building, I needed out quickly. Though without a job, or anything lined up, I was nervous no landlord would rent to me.

I returned to my office, packed up as many of my personal items as I could manage, and walked out. Saying goodbye only to Betty only because I saw her on my way out. I was sad that I never made any connections within the company, scared that I was leaving all that I've known for too many years and felt like I was going to vomit from my fear.

Once I got out of the building I realized how inconvenient it was to have taken the bus. I didn't expect to be carrying so much, including a half-dead house plant, on my way home today. Close to tears, I sat down on the short wall outside the office, setting everything at my feet and called Travis. "Sorry for waking you up again. I –"

"You didn't, actually. I'm on my way to class. What's up?"

I looked at my watch, not having realized it was as late in the morning as it was and the tears started, no longer was I confident enough to hold them back. "I just quit," I squeaked out. "I need a drive but I'll find another way. Go to class."

"Don't be ridiculous. Where are you?" The guilt was compounding, but I needed to get away from the office as quickly as possible.

"The office, just outside the door. Please don't miss class for me."

"I'll be right there." And he was. He drove up to the curb within minutes, ignoring all signs that he wasn't allowed to park there. Car horns blared as he hurriedly got out of the car and ran around to pick up my stuff and put everything carefully in the backseat. I got in the passenger's seat and closed the door then was surprised he opened it back up. He leaned in awkwardly and gave me a hug before getting into his side of the car.

"I desperately want to give you a proper hug right now, but that will need to wait. You are so brave! Tell me what happened."

So I did, quickly, as he drove me home and I demanded he get to class. I took the plant and a few manageable things from his back seat, blew him a kiss and assured him I'd be fine. I already resolved to go to the gym to work off my nerves, and the cake. He promised to call me when he could and to come over after class, before his shift.

I let myself into my apartment and, before a second thought, got changed and escaped to the comfort of the gym. I laughed at the thought as I never in a million years, or forty to be exact, did I ever think the gym would be my safe place or offer comfort. But there I was, a whole new woman who was unemployed and soon to be homeless.

Working out like never before I was starving and looking forward to the recently prepared work lunches that would now be eaten at home. On my walk back home I stopped into see Megan and buy any paper I could with a classified section and job ads. I was newly in search of a job and a home. Megan wasn't working so I quickly grabbed the papers and went home to eat two lunches.

Chapter Nine

I talked with Travis during one of his breaks, reassured him that I was fine alone and that I would be making him dinner for after his school day. Between prep work and while I waited, I dove head first into the real estate listings and then the job listings, alternating between them as I was unsure which should come first.

The oven alerted me to supper being ready just as the intercom sounded. "Hello?" I said into it nervously.

"Just me, Sugarplum. Open up."

"Perfect timing, Travis. Supper is ready." I buzzed to let him in and opened the door slightly, surprised how much better it felt that I knew Mike was in jail. Travis came in as I was setting food on the table. When I turned to get another dish he stopped me with a hug, clearly still favouring his punching hand, and he whispered how gorgeous I was.

I noticed he was holding a bottle of wine in his left hand when he let go and asked if I had wine glasses. "Of course. Top small cupboard, beside the fridge," I instructed as I grabbed the garlic bread to go with the lasagna.

When we sat down across from each other at the small table he raised a wine filled glass and said he was toasting me for a job well quit. "Cheers to that," I said as we clinked glasses and each took hearty sips of the fabulous wine. "Let's dig in, I'm starving."

"Me, too and I hate that I have to work tonight, but I have about an hour. Tell me everything."

I proceeded to and he listened to every word. Even during pauses where I just embraced how wonderful it felt to have a companion to talk to over dinner, he sat and listened. Applauding and groaning in the appropriate places, ensuring I knew he was listening to every single world.

It didn't take as long as it felt in real time to tell the story and it felt so good to have it said it all out loud. I ended with the fact that I already picked up papers to find a new job and place to live when he surprised me with, "Please, stay with me. I'll sleep on the couch as much as I can, you can have my room. Kate will likely be moving out soon and then you can have her room. This isn't up for debate and this isn't the point in our relationship where I'm asking you to move in with me. This is an easy, quick solution to an otherwise crazy and immediate problem."

I listened, groaning and applauding and almost in tears at the appropriate places. I couldn't imagine living with a boy, a man, a boyfriend, so soon, but the arrangement could work.

"Don't tell me now, think about it overnight but remember – Chuck is right below you."

We both shivered at the thought and I promised I would think about it as he rushed out the door to get home before his shift, thanking me for the delicious meal.

After he left and I cleaned up, I decided to meet him at the bar to celebrate that I made a decision. While he was working and I promised myself I wouldn't bother him, I could have another drink and listen to the music. Maybe meet a new friend.

I texted Megan and she decided to join me. Megan arrived first and I joined her at a table in the corner. Soon after Kate joined us, and we declared it a girls night. No boys allowed. When Travis walked by to another table he seemed surprised, but delighted, to see me. After dropping off the drinks to the only other customers in the place, he returned to our table and tried to sit.

We all giggled and refused. Saying we were there to gossip about boys and they weren't allowed to disturb us.

With a peck on my cheek he returned to his place at the bar. I kept glancing over to him as he watched the baseball game playing on the television behind the bar. I felt him peek at me a few times, too but he kept his distance.

I bought Kate a virgin drink to celebrate her new job at the local art gallery and she bought me an alcoholic one in return, to celebrate my job loss. We both treated Megan to a drink, too, celebrating her two new besties!

Unfortunately, they both left early as it was, for them, a work night and I turned to see that I was the lone customer in the bar. Feeling the table was much too big for one, and too far away from the bartender for two, I made my way to a stool.

Pretending to watch the game, too, I asked "What team are we cheering for? Did Jordan get a touch down yet?"

Travis was startled at my presence, not realizing I made it so close to him as he was too absorbed in the game to notice. It was tied in the ninth inning and the Cardinals were at bat. "Are you serious?"

I couldn't hold it back. I broke out in drunken laughter, confessing to know a little more about sports than I was letting on. I was sober enough to see the relief in his body language and giggled, proud I had him going even just for a second.

Leaning over the bar he gave me a kiss and asked where my friends went. "The party poopers had to go home to bed. I was just getting started."

"Well, looks like the weather is keeping other people away so Jack told me to lock up. Want to come upstairs?"

"Weather? It wasn't doing a thing when I came over."

"Apparently it's raining buckets out now. Let's go see."

He came around the bar, helped me down off the stool and went to the front door. Opening it, we could tell it was clearly pouring rain so I was shocked when he pulled me outside. With nothing to protect us, we quickly got soaked as he leaned me against the wall and kissed me. Hard.

As was his penis, I discovered.

We let the rain soak us, right through my white blouse and when his lips left mine and his hand grabbed my ass I whispered "what about the game?"

"What game?" he answered and I knew he, at that moment, could care less about the Cardinals. I tried to lift my leg, to wrap it around his waist like I saw in movies but was quickly reminded of my age and hours at the gym earlier.

"Let's go upstairs." He led the way through the bar, locking up and turning off the open sign.

"Let's go home, roomie." I winked as his smile grew, understanding the meaning behind my words. I made my way up the stairs and he soon joined me.

Although my body was exhausted from the work out, Travis found some new energy within me and turned it on.

Chapter Ten

I moved in with him two days later, giving my notice at the apartment and putting my belongings in storage. Going to the gym daily I was able to firm my soft spots, clear my head and determine that I no longer wanted to work for someone else. I also declined Frank's suggestion of driving an Uber and followed up with him to tell him so by text.

I signed up for yoga classes through the gym, met some fun acquaintances and they convinced me to start a blog about finding myself at forty. It would be like a journal, but with the potential of a monetary twist. Not only would I include affiliate links for products I tested, along with reviews of each, I would start asking for sponsors as I built my following. It was going to be a slow start, that I knew, but it would also help me re-discover myself and my passion for writing.

I started just one week later, naming my blog, Finding Me At 40.

While I was eager to start, I wanted to do things right so wrote down a few topic and title ideas in advance, set up some social media sites and set a schedule for posting every two days and writing after supper. It didn't conflict with my classes at the gym, or take away from time with Travis as he would be going to work then and I would still have the opportunity to take classes if I wanted to.

Looking into all of the options at Travis's college, I hesitated being at the same school as him as I was concerned we'd get sick of each other. I knew I needed to talk to Joey for advice so asked Travis if he could get his number. At first he was jealous, saying he never thought I'd ask him to give me an old crushes number but, after I explained, thought it was a great idea.

With that decided, I also looked for courses I could take online and found one for marketing that I could take on my own time. It didn't cost a lot so I registered right away. Once I did, many emails came in suggesting other courses to compliment and I signed up for a blog writing one. I already had some idea how to write a blog but decided it wouldn't hurt if I was going to make this a long term commitment. And then I sat down to write my first post.

I was surprised and impressed at how easily and quickly the words came to me. I didn't worry so much about audience or censoring, I just let it flow and came up with one thousand words within minutes. I decided I would see if I could write a second just as easily and was shocked when I did. Within the hour I had five rough drafts written and decided that was enough, that I would edit them the next day and see if I still thought they were good enough for readers.

In the meantime, I began searching online for products to recommend in the posts and then navigated to social media to post on my page. Already it received twenty seven new likes from just a few basic posts being shared. I trusted that wouldn't be the amount I'd receive per day but was confident this proved there was a market for me. Or at least a group of people interested enough to share my meme's. I barely even knew what that meant, but wanted to take full advantage of every opportunity.

I joined a few groups filled with middle aged woman, mostly mom groups, and felt a sense of guilt. Maybe, with my being childless, I wouldn't fit in or be able to respond as well as I wanted to with others the same age, but I scrolled through, found some rants I could relate to, and commented. Careful not to spam the group and intent on starting to form relationships as well as better understand what my potential target audience were interested in reading about.

After two hours of screen time, my eyes hurt as much as my fingers so I decided to stretch and work on some yoga poses. One was really kicking my ass and, as I tried to master it, Kate opened the door and burst into laughter while I collapsed, the pose still beating me. I soon joined her in the laughing and realized that I would turn that incident into my next blog post.

We chatted for a while, she told me she was moving out and invited me to take over her room. She explained that her job was wonderful and she really felt confident that it was time to find her own place. With the baby coming, Travis's place was too small as it was so she decided it was better to go out on her own again and get settled. I pleaded with her to stay, trying to come up with any good excuse to keep her close as I wasn't ready to be "living with my boyfriend" yet.

Kate seemed to understand as she said I was welcome to stay with her at any time. She explained that she was basically just across the street, not going far, and would give me a key. "I figure I may need to call you to babysit or something and it would be easier if you had your own key."

"Thank you for your faith in me. I'm not sure I'd be much of a sitter though, never being around kids, or babies, but I'm looking forward to meeting him or her."

"You'll do fine. Especially if you're stretching yourself like this now." She laughed and pointed to my yoga mat. "Want to help me start packing?"

"So soon? When do you move out? Have you even told Travis?"

"I'll stay the night here but the place is furnished and empty so I said I'd be moved in tomorrow. I had to pay a bit more than I wanted, but it's a great location and I was desperate. I may also be a tad crazy but my doctor hasn't checked for that yet."

We laughed as I rolled up my mat and put it in the corner of the living room. "Why don't you put that in here? Assuming you'll be giving Travis back his bedroom, mean?"

"Yeah, I guess you're right. It's his place so he should have the bigger spot with his clothes already in it. I don't want to make you feel like I'm rushing you out."

"It was my idea! And it's just a mat. Come on. I don't have much but have learned it's easier to put in boxes than in garbage bags. What are you doing tomorrow?"

I figured out the meaning behind the question quickly enough to reply, "Helping a friend move, I guess." I decided this would be a reason to skip the gym, walking the boxes over a block and across a busy street.

"Oh, one second. I know just what will fill that box." I ran to Travis room and dug through a box of my own to find my first gift for baby. A onesie with a baby elephant on the front. I held it up and tried to imagine a human in it but it seemed an impossible feat.

Bringing it to Kate she welled up immediately, took it and cried into it as she sat on the edge of the bed. "Oh, Megan, thank you! Elephants have always brought me luck, I hope it does this time, too."

"Me, too," I said as I sat beside her and put an arm around her, letting her sob into my shoulder understanding that it was much more than my present causing the tears.

Chapter Eleven

Kate moved out and Travis took back his room, saying I didn't have to leave, but I insisted. It was just too soon. Over the next several weeks I launched my blog and began getting traction as well as free goodies of all different varieties. With the target audience of my blog being older ladies, most of the items were anti-aging creams, serums and even some lingerie that was supposed to be designed for my target audience. I wasn't sure how I felt about it all, but decided to test it all out and provide an honest review it. Even if I received the items for free, if I wouldn't recommend it I would say so. If it was absolutely horrible, I'd let the company know and decide on my actions based on their response. It wouldn't be ethical otherwise.

On the one month anniversary of my surprisingly successful blog I surprised my audience with the launch of a YouTube channel. This would be focused on reviews but also to answer some of my follower's questions from the blog. It was nerve wracking as I never imagined I'd be brave enough to show my face for something like that, but was loving the adventure. I wasn't quite making enough financially to pay for even half the rent yet, and my savings were quickly dwindling, so I needed to do something and the courses all suggested videos were the key.

Not yet having the subscribers or watch time to go live, I navigated my way to find "shorts" which would allow a brief live video. I first shot one of me introducing myself and my site, explaining what my videos would aim to do and how often I would post one. I watched it several times before posting and then prepared myself to go live on my Facebook page to invite them over to the channel. It was 1 PM on a Wednesday, seemed as good a time as any to go live and not get a large audience but to help get over my fear.

Taking a deep breath and looking for the twelfth time in the mirror I hit the record button on my computer. It didn't seem to be working, nothing changed on my monitor so when my cell phone rang I answered it. "Hey baby. How's school?"

I knew it was Travis and was excited to tell him of my plan for the day. "It's ok. I can't believe I only have a month to go!"

"I'm so proud of you, hot stuff. And I have some exciting news of my own. I got some lingerie today for review and I'm wearing it right now. I'm hoping that you can unwrap me before you go to work."

There was some hustling and movement before he replied, "Sorry, Annabelle. I should have mentioned. You were on speaker and I'm with the guys."

"Did I make them hard? Did I make you hard?" I was giddy and getting horny at the idea. Wearing lingerie during the day really got me going. "I'm getting wet, baby."

"Oh goodness, Annabelle. Should I run home now?"

"Oh yes, please. Oh shit! No no no no no!" I glanced at my monitor and realized I was on video, there must have been a delay before recording and I didn't realize. My viewership was doubling by the second. "I have to let you go." I hung up quickly, with no explanation and turned back to the camera.

"Wow, hi everyone! I bet you weren't expecting that type of party but I'm glad you all came…er ….I'm glad you joined me. No, um, let's forget all that. I'm actually here to announce my YouTube Channel – Losing It Past 40. And trust me, if you liked what you just heard I'm sure there will be more of it. I'm not so technically enabled and have to admit, I make mistakes. This one time I answered a call on video while I was undressing and put on a show. Thankfully, it was someone I was dating and not a relative."

I rambled for ten minutes, trying to make the first two awkward introductory minutes seem in the far distance and maybe unbelievable. I lost viewers, absolutely, but enough stayed with me until the end. I signed off with a promise of a gift card to one of the viewers, not even realizing I was going to do that. I explained that they needed to invite a new friend to the group, or at least to watch the video and as soon as it reached one hundred views I would draw from those who participated.

I got a notification an hour later that my video had one thousand views and I screamed with delight and then quickly put a pillow over my face to muffle the scream and did it again. Then I called Travis and, though I knew he was in class, I had to share the news with him.

He answered, whispering into the phone and I apologized then quickly told him the news. He screamed, too. Delighted and thrilled that I was gaining momentum so quickly. He said class was just finishing up but he was going to run an errand and then be home to celebrate. He would pick up dinner on the way.

That decided, and a gift card winner to announce, I turned back to the computer to see the page likes almost doubled. I checked my YouTube account to see the one video had gained hundreds of views, too and my channel, with the lone video copied from Facebook and lone short, was up to eighty two. Making the decision not to edit my live video, the conversation with Travis really wasn't terrible and was exactly what my target audience expected, I chalked it up to a happy accident and uploaded the full video to the channel.

Logging onto my page I wrote a post about going live again in less than five minutes to announce not just one winner, but two, of $50 Amazon gift cards. Turning away from the ever increasing likes and comments on that post, I worked at filling in all the names of my page likes into an online generator and then went live again, knowing now there would be a delay.

Once I was on the screen I saw viewers start joining me. I waited a beat, welcoming everyone back and then when I saw twenty people watching I switched to showing them the circle with everyone's names. Not full names, of course, as some may have wished to remain anonymous. Clicking the icon to spin the wheel I was delighted to see some people saying hi and some compliments about my posts. I reminded them to always check back on Tuesdays as I decided to release each post that day. If I had another review for that week, I'd post it on Friday.

With the first name chosen I saw many people post congratulatory notes for Chelsea K. and many more join in on the viewing. At one point I noticed I was up to forty eight and thought that was decent.

"Ok, one more winner to name but I wanted to thank you all for sharing, commenting and supporting this endeavour. As my page and blog, and now Channel grow, I promise to do more giveaways and am open to suggestions on what you want me to give away."

I was shocked to see a man in the group named Michael comment that he wanted me to give away my body. It took me a second and then I realized who it was and tried to continue my video without causing too much disruption as I worked to remove his comment and block him. I couldn't believe he'd be able to stalk me from his jail cell, but I had no doubt it was him.

I quickly drew the other name and signed off, distracting myself with contacting the winners about their gift cards until Travis came home.

Chapter Twelve

Travis wasn't much later after I busied myself with gifting the cards and doing a bit more marketing. Logging back onto my blog I noticed lots of spam comments mixed with valid ones so set up a filter. It would be annoying to have to approve all of the comments, but it would be worth it.

When he arrived he carried to bags of Chinese food from a place I've never been. "You will be amazed then, Annabelle. You deserve the best so I got the best. And I got Jack to cover for me tonight so we don't have to rush."

He was right. The food was the best I had ever eaten and I loved that I was eating out of the boxes, sharing with him without either of us minding. There would be many firsts with Travis and I was glad this was one of them.

Once completely stuffed that we couldn't eat anymore, Travis reached into his back pocket and brought out an envelope. "That's not all, my dear. You deserve to be celebrated again and again. I'm so proud of your bravery and determination to make this work. I do hope someday soon you'll join me in my bedroom and be my live-in partner instead of just a roommate."

He handed me the envelope and leaned in to steal a kiss at the same time. I opened it hesitantly and was shocked to see it was a gift certificate for Tara's Glama Shots. Reading further I thought it said a photo shoot at a boudoir photo studio. It couldn't be so after looking it over a few times and not seeing anything else I asked.

"Yes, baby, you understand correctly. I thought with the new lingerie, your new found confidence and tighter body, it would make a great topic for your blog. And, of course, I'll buy all the pictures. Please baby? She has an opening Saturday, I booked it tentatively but wanted to be sure you were free."

"Saturday? Nude photos? Me?" I wasn't speechless often, but I couldn't form a sensible sentence in that moment, no matter how hard I tried. I had seen some shots before, in magazines and such, but they were skinny. The models were young. They were sexy. "Oh, I don't think so." I finally found my words.

"Please, baby? Tara said I was allowed to go in with you if you want. She has someone available to do your hair and makeup, and she knows who you are, so gave me a discount. Don't decide now, just think about it."

The Chinese food was making itself known by forming a pit in my stomach which felt like the size of the Grand Canyon. I excused myself to the bathroom, embarrassed that Chinese food always revisited so quickly, and then I remembered I had the new lingerie on and didn't imagine it would be easy to get out of, as silly as that seemed.

I made it out in time and decided quickly to have a shower after. A notification dinged on my phone informing me I reached 1000 viewers on my YouTube video and quickly decided to put the lingerie back on, feeling better and forgetting temporarily about the gift certificate in the excitement.

Exiting the bathroom I saw that Travis had already cleaned up the leftovers and lit a candle in his room. Romantic music played as he invited me in, thrilled to see my new wardrobe.

"Ooo la la. Come here, baby."

He pulled me onto the bed, and as he explored the soft material of my new lingerie I undressed him and we celebrated several times before falling asleep, naked in each other's arms.

The next morning I started moving my things into his room. He already left for class and I decided it was silly not to be sleeping so well every night. I hoped he felt the same way.

Without checking again on my views or anything to do with the side hustle, I escaped to the gym for two hours of exercise and mental health. The distraction would be good and keep me busy. It was strange though, as when I walked in the person at the desk seemed genuinely excited to see me. Usually she would just smile and maybe say a hello. This time was different.

"Annabelle! How are you?"

"I'm good thanks....Tanya." I had to squint to read her name tag, embarrassed to never have known her name before. "How are you?"

"I'm still in stitches. My mom sent me a blog she's been reading and I loved it. I was shocked to find out it's you! You're hilarious! And so damn brave. I could never do that, just quit a job and write. I've always wanted to be a writer, but needed something more practical and stable to pay the bills, you know?"

I did know but this young twenty-something purple haired skinny girl wasn't the right target for my posts. What was she doing reading my stuff and talking about my bravery? She had all the confidence in the world and it showed. And then I realized, people could have very well said the same about me, even before I turned forty.

I was a great employee, polite and dressed professionally. No one really knew me at all to know how scared I was. To know that every time I even went to the hairdressers I was a nervous wreck. That I bit the inside of my cheek and stared at the wall or mirror, seeing nothing at all but hoping to avoid awkward small talk with the stranger. Tanya made me see things in a whole new light again and it was one I could take advantage of.

My target audience wasn't necessarily made up of forty year old women who had much more confidence than me, but a mix of them and some still searching for themselves and finding their spark, too. I wasn't necessarily the joke of my readers, but their inspiration, and that dumbfounded me.

"Tanya, thank you. Your words mean a tremendous deal to me and I hope you'll remain a fan and find your niche, too."

I continued to the locker room, noticing I was a bit taller and walking with a greater stride than before. While noticeable, it also seemed more natural.

I killed it on the machines and enjoyed every second of it. After showering I dared catch more than a glance of myself in the full length mirror and said aloud, "To hell with it. I'm doing it!" At that time of day there were not many in the locker room but those who did clearly heard me as they repeated my words, clearly not knowing what my 'it' was but possibly having an 'it' all their own. I smiled at them all and told them they needed to do it and soon. No one else was going to do it for them.

Each one of them laughed with me which made me feel great. It didn't matter to me that I was still naked, the towel wrapped around some bits and then that was too much. In unity, we all took our towels off as if we agreed to protest the cotton without even talking about it. And I didn't care! Just as easily as I started finding fans for my blog, I shrugged off that prudish feeling of needing to always be covered.

After getting dressed and leaving the gym I texted Travis - I am good for Saturday. ;)

He called me as soon as he must have received it and I could hear the smile in his voice. The pride.

Chapter Thirteen

I wrote a blog Friday about my plans for Saturday, still confident I was going through with it and letting my fans know I'd be reviewing the experience and possibly posting a photo or two. I linked back to Tara's Glama and got a comment from her almost instantly.

Can't wait to see you! I have some great shots in mind. :)

Instead of making me nervous it inspired me to complete an Internet search for pose ideas. While I knew she was the professional and would do what was best for me, I wanted to know what to expect. I searched her site as well as Facebook page to find so many happy clients and dozens of fabulous photos, but then I went a step further and looked up some of her competitors' sites for different ideas. I found a few and printed them out. Folding them and putting them into my purse, I then packed a little bag of items I wanted to take, including my new lingerie I received for review. When I put them in, I remembered the time I dropped my purse at the bar and all the condoms flew out. That memory, now that I could laugh about it, would make for another great blog post. I thought that would add a special touch to my Tuesday blog.

Once satisfied, I went down to the bar to meet Megan for a few drinks. I didn't want to have too many but did feel I deserved to celebrate the week. She was there waiting for me and had drinks on the table already. She stood to hug me, and then we took our seats. I couldn't hold back, I blurted out my plans for Saturday and she just laughed, said she already knew.

"Oh? Did Travis tell you?"

"No, hunny, you did. You told the whole world!" It took me a second to sort out that she was talking about my blog. I loved that so many were reading it but never once thought people I knew would be, too. I should have, Megan was my biggest supporter through all of this. It was like I had known her for years instead of just months.

"So… then… you know all about the excitement in my life, but I don't know what's happening in yours."

"Not much, actually. The kids are growing and driving me mad. Work is steady which is great. I have a new fab friend I'm so jealous of and want to be like. I will tell you this though, your blog has certainly helped me in the bedroom. Your antics are driving my own sex drive up a notch and the husband isn't complaining."

We giggled like young girls on the playground, both so happy to have found each other and improve each other's lives.

Travis joined us briefly while on his break and it felt great. Megan and Travis got along well and kissing in front of her didn't seem wrong as I knew she'd be bringing back the heat to her own house later.

Soon after, Megan announced that she should go home and I let Travis know I was going upstairs. My appointment was at 11 AM and I wanted a goodnights sleep to help reduce the bags under my eyes. I did suggest to Travis that he wake me for a late night delight as it would help me sleep even better to which he eagerly agreed.

I slept easily and was pleasantly delighted when I woke to his lips on mine. I had started sleeping naked and was enjoying the benefits of feeling his skin against mine. Arching my back as he made his way into my folds with his tongue, I was woke quickly and participating in seconds. Without much talk, he elevated my blood pressure and heart rate to levels that thrilled me. Once we were both finished I wobbled my way to the bathroom to urinate. When I sat down I wondered about the date, not really watching the calendar as much as when I worked in an office, and, exhausted, couldn't sort out the day. I wiped, shrugged, crawled back into bed and just as quickly as Travis woke me, I fell back to sleep.

The alarm sounded at 9 AM, waking us both. It was Saturday!

I had a nice long, hot shower finishing with a bit of cold water to energize me, and dressed. Tara recommended comfortable clothes that were easy to get off and change back into so I went with jogging pants and a hoodie, with just basic panties and bra. I let my hair dry naturally and left it down, knowing the stylist would find that easiest.

Travis drove me to her studio and we went in together but I told him I'd rather surprise him with the pictures. He was supportive, though clearly disappointed, which I found sweet. Tara met us and introduced herself as well as her make-up and hair team, two lovely ladies who were apparently fans of my blog, too. I said goodbye to Travis and Tara asked him to give them four hours.

With only ladies left in the room, Tara said she normally had her clients fill in a questionnaire but, with the circumstances, was fine with just asking the questions while she got ready if I was comfortable with that. I agreed and took a seat for the hair and make-up team to get started. Tara sat across from me and started off with just some general, friendly chat and then asked one I wasn't ready for. "When was your last period? I only ask because we take certain measures if you're menstruating now, to ensure our clothes are protected, of course." She seemed comfortable asking but it felt intrusive. I understood why she would need to ask, of course, and wouldn't be there if it was time of the month for me, though she had no way of knowing that.

"Umm..." and then I suddenly realized it had been a while. "What's the date today?"

"March 12th."

"I guess it's been a couple of months, but I just started birth control and am 'of that age'." I couldn't age Tara, she seemed younger than me but could have been older.

"Oh dear, we're all at that age. I'm forty-seven." Tara confessed.

"Wow! You look great for forty-seven. I thought you were younger than me. I just turned forty and my life got crazy."

"It does that sometimes. I'm glad your crazy brought you to me. Travis, he's some catch! I wish I was that lucky when I turned forty. All I got was a cake and a divorce."

We all laughed like we were old friends and I was distracted enough, answering the questions, that I didn't notice the transformation being made before my eyes. When I looked in the mirror I saw myself but a much better, seemingly younger, version of me. I saw what I felt – confidence, passion, spirit and showed it with a big ass smile.

"Ready to get dressed," Tara asked. "You can change behind that curtain, there's a few options hung up there for you. If they are too big just let me know, I may have other sizes."

It was delightful to hear the phrase 'too big' instead of too small and an even better feeling to have that be exactly the case. My time at the gym, and with Travis, was paying off big time. Or was that slimming time?

I found an outfit that I felt comfortable in, and excited to get the show started, and came out from behind the curtain straight into the studio.

Chapter Fourteen

Tara was the only one remaining in the room and she had her camera in hand and her lighting ready for the first few photos. It seemed impulsive, but she took some shots of me coming out, much braver than I thought I'd be dressed in lingerie and heels in front of another woman. Somehow this woman made me feel like an equal, maybe even a beauty to behold and, most importantly, comfortable.

She guided me to an empty claw foot bathtub beside a window she assured me no one could see in through. I shivered, out of nervousness more than cold, as she had the room set at a perfect temperature. "Just a bit chilled to make your colour pop and your nipples hard." She said it in a way that made me trust her professionalism even more.

The hours and a bit flew bit in a wink. With a few costume changes, likely hundreds of poses and even more clicks of her camera, we heard the knock and Travis announce his arrival in what felt like minutes. During our very therapeutic chat, I felt was needed for both of us, I asked Tara about surprising Travis with a little sneak peek when he got back and she agreed. She explained that she didn't usually let men come in but, under these circumstances, she'd make an exception. She did ask that I not include the exception in any review or future blog I might write and I agreed.

Tara welcomed Travis in and said he was welcome to come back to the studio. The look on his face was remarkable and Tara captured that forever. I was sprawled out on the bed, posed just so in my new lingerie and I could tell he was struggling to refrain from joining me. Tara seemed to notice it, too as she excused herself, promising to just be a moment.

Once she was out of the room, he bolted towards me and kissed me with such abandon I didn't even notice the flashes from the camera. Tara apparently snuck back in, caught us in action, and snuck back out. The next time she entered she announced her arrival and we separated, Travis quickly taking his spot a few feet away from the bed.

"I have an idea. One that you may or may not like. I'm free for a bit before I have to get my kids and I wanted to try something different. Travis, do you mind being in a few shots?"

I didn't know what to think. My nerves were on fire again, not to mention my loins which I hoped weren't soiling her sheets. Travis stood, speechless, but not for long. "What would I wear?"

"Whatever you have on is fine. I don't have a male wardrobe on hand. Even if you want to just take off your shirt…" she started to say as she turned to prepare something and then noticed he was already down to his boxers. "I take that as a yes," Tara concluded.

For the next twenty minutes, Tara had us position ourselves in different ways with the rule that we weren't allowed to touch. She explained that it was the anticipation that made a photo, not the act itself. By the time we were done the room felt like it was 90° F.

Travis put on his clothes, careful not to catch his erection in his zipper, and I went behind the curtain to put on mine. It seemed silly to do so now, with both people in the room seeing me in very compromising positions already but I figured my clothes were there anyway and it would give me a minute to cool off.

Tara busied herself with turning off lights and packing away her camera. She shook each of our hands when we were leaving and said we were welcome back anytime. I gave her my coupon and promised to let her know when my review was posted, assuring her it would be flattering.

She asked me to simply be honest or else it wouldn't be authentic and said she would be in touch later in the week to discuss which shots I wanted printed and how.

Travis drove us home, barely able to stop touching me if only just to hold my hand. I felt the best I've felt in a very long time and was ready to take on the world. I did want to get the blog written soon after my experience, but I also knew Travis was about to keep me busy for a little while and I wasn't about to say no to that. What Tara and Travis didn't know was that I kept my lingerie on, even though it was the same set Travis had seen, it was all I had with me.

I also put the very puzzling moment in the back of my head for the time being as I let Travis take full advantage of my mood for over an hour. Spent from all the activity and the busy day, we agreed to order take out for supper and that, while I wrote my blog, he would run to get it. "Obviously I didn't play you hard enough if you still have that amount of energy."

"Oh, girl, you sure did but I'm starving now and want to give you peace to write in. Once I eat, though, we'll talk about round two." He left and I sat at the table with my laptop. While it was booting up I made myself a Maple Chai Latte and returned, with it in hand, to the table. I clicked on the email program first and then went to log into my website, taking a sip of tea as I waited for both to load. When I looked at the amount of emails I had waiting I spit my tea all over the screen. There were 986 emails loading, all notifications of a comment on my blog.

After cleaning up the screen and keyboard, as well as taking a deep breath, I looked again. Some were spam comments, but many were actually positive words of encouragement as well as stories of their own. Clicking over to the website I quickly approved some of the more generic comments, deleted the spam ones and vowed to read the stories before posting them. Before I read them I did want to write my blog post. Although it wouldn't go live until Tuesday, I wanted to recap everything while it was fresh.

And it was at that moment I remembered the puzzling moment that was stuck in the back of my mind.

About half way through the session, when Tara came to help me pose just so, her arm brushed slightly against my nipple and it was hard to not react. The slight touch seemed unusually painful. She appeared to pause just for a brief moment, but continue without bringing attention to my tension. I did note that she seemed more careful not to touch the area and suddenly looked like she had a secret she wasn't sharing.

The moment passed and I tried to block, it but it seemed significant enough to tell Travis. I left that moment out of my post and wrote six hundred twenty three words in no time. Deciding to leave it to read over the next day, I returned to start reading the longer comments. I read through three amazing stories and approved two, immediately. They were hilarious, not too personal and fit the target audience of my blog.

Before closing my email I checked again to see another thirty four comments, one of which was from a company. I clicked on it, feeling guilty for prioritizing it, but was glad I did.

Reading it over three times before I heard Travis at the door, I was dumbfounded. He came in, set the food on the counter, said something to me I didn't register and then came to my side. He began massaging my shoulders as I just sat frozen staring at the screen.

"Annabelle? Are you ok?"

"Look," I managed to get out and point to the screen. Travis read over my shoulder and realized the meaning behind my reaction.

"Annabelle, that is amazing! A talk show? You're going to do it, right? Think about how much that would mean; not only to you and growing your audience base but to the people who need your stories and haven't found you yet."

"I will have to think about it. I never wanted all this attention, I just needed an outlet and a way to keep busy, but I think you're right." I closed my laptop and moved it aside. "I'm starving. Let's eat!"

Chapter Fifteen

I decided to wait until Monday to write the company back, using Sunday to go through some more comments and watch a movie with Travis. Once the movie was over I asked him to read over my blog to give me his thoughts. I also mentioned, once he was done, that I needed to talk to him about something. The idea of opening up to something so personal, which had the potential of being serious, was terrifying, but I needed to pull up my socks and be honest if the relationship was going to last, like I hoped. He laughed and gasped throughout the reading and then came to sit beside me on the couch.

"It's great! I love that you experienced so much. What a memorable time and I just know your readers will adore it. You should warn Tara that she'll get even busier in the coming months."

"You think so? She is wonderful, truly, and you are an awesome boyfriend to encourage me to do that. I wouldn't have done it without you."

"I know. You deserve that and much, much more. I'm trying to convince Kate to go there for her pregnancy photo shoot. She's more nervous than you were, it seemed, but I think hearing about your experience will convince her to go."

"I think that's a fabulous idea! I'm sure she's going to need a baby shower soon, why don't we plan one and get her a gift certificate to go to Tara. If she refuses, I'm sure I can find a fan to give it away to."

"You're so sweet," Travis leaned over to kiss me. "Now what else did you want to talk about?"

"A bit I left out of my post because it's too personal. I didn't even tell Tara."

"Something serious?"

"I don't know yet. I guess it has the potential to be. I wanted your opinion."

He held my hand tightly. "Whatever it is, we can figure it out."

I wasn't sure where to start – the questionnaire and not knowing when my last period was, the feeling when she brushed against my breast, that I may have been late taking my birth control a few nights. So I blurted out, "My boobs hurt." Yup, that about summed it up.

Only he responded in awkward laughter and moved away from me. "Sorry, I didn't even realize I was squishing them."

"No, I don't mean right now. You weren't, they were OK, get back over here please." He moved back closer, turning to sit on the couch so he could face me and take both of my hands as I mirrored him. "I meant, in general, they are more sensitive lately. Tara brushed against them and it felt like she was squeezing them with pliers. My nipples, too, seem so sensitive. Like even when I put a bra on they get ticklish."

"Should you go see a doctor?" He seemed genuinely concerned and that tugged on my heart strings, though I could tell he wasn't thinking of the most obvious answer. I really wasn't either, tried to reason with myself that even without the birth control getting pregnant wasn't likely. Which was somewhat more concerning. Although cancer didn't run in the family, it never really had to. Though I also didn't want to think about the more serious alternatives, I figured I would rule out the easier possibilities first.

"Maybe let's start with a pregnancy test, or three." I watched him closely, trying to gauge his maturity in that moment and was thrilled to see the possibility excited him.

"I'll go get some now." He jumped up and was out the door before he realized he didn't have his shoes on. I laughed when he came back in and put them on the wrong feet. "It doesn't matter, I'll be right back."

"Please don't go to Megan's store." I rushed to say. Whether or not the test was positive, I didn't want her to worry or start asking questions until I knew more.

The door closed but I heard a muffled, "Got it, not Megan's store, as he went.

While he was away I opened my laptop to read some more stories, but found myself opening a new post for my blog and writing about the idea of being pregnant at forty. It was more of a private journal entry than anything. I was hoping that if I put the words on a page they would seem too ludicrous to be true. By the time I ended the post I was actually kind of excited about the idea of being pregnant though quickly laughed. Not only was I too old, I was unemployed and homeless. There was no way I was ready to raise a kid with a boyfriend half my age and a relationship only a few months old.

And then it hit me harder.

What if I was pregnant and it wasn't his? With the timeline, it was quite possible Chuck was the father, if there was a father at all, and I cringed. Travis was standing next to me and I didn't even hear him come in. I hoped he didn't realize how stressed I was or that, if he did, he would just chalk it up to the possibility of my being pregnant.

I clicked save on the blog post quickly to ensure he didn't see even the title and closed my laptop.

"Welcome home. How did that go?"

"Easy enough. I got two of the same brand, and three more of different brands. One says it will even tell us how pregnant you are, if you are at all. The cashier looked at me funny, but I went out of my way to go to a different store so will easily avoid that one in the future. Which one would you like to try first? Do you need to pee? Should I get you some water?" I stood and took his hands in mine as he opened the bag and looked in. He was rambling, his nervousness was obvious, and I could only stop him with a kiss. I took the bag out of his hands and led him to the couch.

I set the bag down on the floor, went to get us both a glass of water and, as the water was running I heard my phone receive a constant stream of notifications. I set the water filled glasses down on the coffee table, turned to get my phone from the dining room table and swore loudly when I looked at it.

In my haste, or numbness, or from being startled, whatever the reason I published my lasted post instead of just saving it. I was mortified. I signed back into my laptop, onto my site and quickly made that post private again but noticed it already had fifty three comments. "Oh God no!"

"What's wrong now? I can't take much more today."

"My post, I published it."

"Well, ok, so you posted your review a couple of days early. Your fans will get it."

"No, I wrote a new one. While you were gone. I… it was… I was just writing a journal entry, but wrote it on my blog and hit publish instead of save." I looked back at Travis who was still on the couch and then back at my blog, scrolling to the bottom to make sure I only thought about the questionable father worry and didn't write it. "Thank God for that small miracle!"

"Which one is that?"

He was standing behind me now, reading some of what I wrote. I quickly closed it, relieved I did only think about the father status, but not wanting him to read what I wrote. And then immediately felt guilty because so many strangers already did read it. At least I hoped they were all strangers. The fact that my phone wasn't yet ringing was a good sign.

I went and grabbed my glass of water, guzzled it down and then grabbed Travis's half full one and guzzled that, too. I needed something stronger, but would have to refrain until I knew for sure.

I grabbed a test randomly from the bag and made my way to the bathroom. Travis followed, asking if it was OK for him to come in with me. "I'll leave the door open, you choose where you sit or stand." I didn't want to be alone yet struggled with the idea of not being the only one who knew the results.

Travis sat on the edge of the bathtub and I pulled down my pants, easily peeing in the direction of the unwrapped stick and all over my hand. I placed it on the corner of the sink, stood, wiped and then washed my hands before pulling up my pants.

"And now we wait."

Chapter Sixteen

Kate walked in while we were still waiting out the minute. Travis was too slow to close the door and I couldn't stop staring at the stick waiting for the pink or blue line to appear.

"I just saw your blog. Are you ok?"

Travis formed the words first, "We don't know anything yet for sure. Can you please give us some privacy?"

"Oh, yes, of course, and you have my support, too. I brought some of my extra tests over, too. I'll just leave them here and go to my old room, unless, is that still Annabelle's room?" She put a bag filled with tiny boxes on the floor in the doorway.

"No, go there, please. Annabelle's with me now. We'll let you know when we need you and thank you." He was short with her, which was odd to hear, but understandable under the circumstances.

Then it was time.

I closed my eyes, took a deep breath and Travis got up to stand beside me. We held hands and I reached out my free hand to carefully pick up the stick and bring it to our line of sight.

Two lines were coloured pink. Faded but visible. I let out my breath slowly, it seemed no oxygen was left in the room.

"'This can't be right. I'm forty years old and weren't even trying."

Travis squeezed my hand tight and suggested I take another. "Maybe one with that shows how many weeks."

I did need to pee again, the nerves punching my bladder like they were mad at it. "I guess so. But what if…"

"We'll worry about if's once we're sure." He dug into the bag and pulled out another one while I took off my pants and sat on the toilet. Immediately I started peeing, just from reflex, and opened my legs wider so he could hold it this time. I stared at him, in disbelief, shock, saying silent prayers that the first test malfunctioned. While we talked briefly about kids when we were first dating, we never thought it would be such a serious topic so soon. Or at least I didn't think it even needed to be mentioned again. I was old, and my eggs were too dry said the doctor, though in more medically acceptable terms, and I was on the pill.

Travis held the stick under my stream until it was only a trickle and then set it on the sink and washed his hands. "This one says five minutes. What do you think about taking another in the meantime to distract us? Do you have some pee left in you?"

I laughed. My chuckle was strained and nervous, sounding unnatural, but his question made me realize how ready I was to go again. He held the stick again, a different brand again and I managed to pee enough and he set that on the counter, too.

We washed our hands and heard Kate making noise in the other room. On one hand, it would be awesome for Kate's child to have a cousin so close in age. We'd have playdates together, hang out together during the day. I could even watch her baby when she went back to work.

My mind was already planning things I didn't even think would be possible. I laughed again, so hard I began to cry and I sat back on the toilet, ensuring the seat was closed.

"We'll get through this, whatever the outcome. It would be kind of neat for Kate to have a niece or nephew the same age as her little one! And we'd be able to watch hers when she goes back to work. They'll be so close."

My tears grew bigger and my laughter louder. I could not believe we were so in sync with our thoughts already. Kate appeared with a glass of water and was polite enough not to ask anything. It did appear that she was trying to sneak a peek at the tests lined up on the counter, but I stood in her way. Even if I was pregnant I wasn't sure I'd be keeping it. Or, for that matter, if he or she would keep me.

After many glasses of water and seven tests in total we were convinced the first one wasn't defective and just stared at each other. It seemed we were miles away while still touching and I blame myself for that. I just never imagined I would have a family. Without my own parents to help, I wasn't sure how I would manage.

"Are you ready to leave the bathroom?"

I laughed at the question as I was eager to sit somewhere other than on the toilet. I was also tired of staring at the bathroom wall and realized there was much to talk about. As I still couldn't find my voice, or maybe it was because I was terrified what I would say, I simply opened the door and made my way to the bedroom where I laid down. Staring at the ceiling, nervous to even look at Travis, I asked if he would join me and he did.

We held hands but didn't say a word for a long time. When our stomachs growled from hunger we both laughed. "I smell bacon. Is Kate still here?"

It was a long time, seemed longer than it actually was, but we were impressed that Kate waited it out and then presented us with breakfast for supper in bed. We both sat up, thanked her and I told her the tests were positive.

She hopped and yelled with delight as we ravenously devoured our respective plates. Between mouthfuls I thanked her for her excitement, but reminded her there were a lot of factors that I was still considering and made her promise to not tell a soul. Then I asked if she could leave Travis and me alone to discuss things.

"Of course. I need to go home anyway, but call me if you need anything, really. I support your decision no matter what."

She took our plates back to the kitchen and we decided to leave the bed and talk in the living room where it was more comfortable.

We talked until the room was dark without a decision being made other than scheduling a doctor's appointment as soon as possible. He vowed to come with me no matter the day or hour which I greatly appreciated. He also said he would support me in whatever I decided, but that wasn't fair. Assuming it was his baby, too, we both had a stake in this. We would figure it out.

We went to bed and simply held each other, our hands instinctively resting on my stomach as if to protect whatever it was growing inside.

Chapter Seventeen

The first thing I did the next morning was call my doctor's office. I begged for the earliest appointment available, explaining that while it wasn't an emergency that warranted a hospital visit, it was urgent. She scheduled me for the first appointment the next day and I thanked her. Though it was earlier in the day than I would have liked, especially if Travis planned to come, it was a sacrifice I had to make.

That done, I turned to my laptop and brought up a job search engine. If I was pregnant and we were going to have the little one, I needed some income. With Travis nearing the end of his course, he, too would be on the hunt for a job that paid better than bartending, but he would have documents to show his skill level. He would also have twenty other classmates with the same degree looking for similar jobs. He was on his own for that and assured me the school had some job options available for those graduating near or at the top of his class and he seemed confident he was there.

Taking a deep breath I completed the filters to be relevant to my location and credentials though hesitated with the location. I could essentially move wherever the job took me, but would Travis come with me? Too many unknowns to make a final decision, I quickly saved some of the job options that would be relevant and then switched to my own site and opened my email.

One thousand emails awaited me which was shocking. What was most surprising was the one I had starred that was waiting for me at the very top. In all the chaos I forgot all about the invitation to be on a talk show. Scared, nervous, wanting to stay hidden and inconspicuous, I was dumbfounded that I picked up the phone and dialed the number in the email. It rang only once, not even giving me the chance to clear my throat or think it through. "Lucy Ball's Studio: Where even women have balls. How may I direct your call?"

My voice came out crackly and weak as I admitted to not knowing who I was to speak with. "I'm Annabelle, I write the Losing It blog. Someone emailed me –"

"Annabelle! Oh my God! Annabelle! I adore you. I want to say so much, but Lucy told me to put you right through to her if you called. We weren't sure you would. One second! I'll get her."

I heard some squeals in the background as the phone was apparently set on the desk. They didn't even put me on hold, but I didn't wait long, either. "Annabelle? Lucy Ball here. I want you on my show. No, I need you on it. When can you come in to talk?"

"I'm free this afternoon."

"Yes, perfect! Let's do lunch. Meet me at Deeno's? Wait, no, I'll send my car. Where will you be at 11:30?"

I gave her my address, or rather Travis's address, and told her I'd be waiting outside for her arrival. Not only was it more convenient, I was still spooked by the idea of Mike just showing up even though I knew he must still be in jail.

I went outside at 11:15, dressed to impress, I hoped, and eager to show my confidence even if I didn't feel it. The car arrived promptly at 11:30 and I went to open the door but was told to stop. The driver was going to open it for me. I sure wasn't used to such royal treatment!

Sitting in the back I distracted myself with light conversation with the driver and trying to decipher the use of all the buttons I didn't dare touch. Thankfully the car ride was short or else I would have had to use the one I couldn't figure out.

Lucy was waiting and opened my door before the driver could. He quickly explained that he would return as soon as Lucy let him know. It seemed unreal to me that a podcaster would hire a driver, but would soon find out all about the perks of the public life and the success of good timing.

There wasn't much fanfare as we made our way to her reserved table and I breathed a sigh of relief that voices of podcasts weren't as recognizable as faces of television shows. Blog writers even less so. We started with pleasantries and orders but, as the waiter returned to the kitchen with our requests, Lucy jumped right in.

"I need you on my show. I think what you're doing with your blog is brilliant and is reaching an audience not many have been able to tap into as well as you have. I know you're new to this and still getting your feet wet but that's even more of a reason to be a guest." She continued with topics she wanted to discuss and bragging about her own show until the food arrived. As soon as my chicken parmesan was set before me I had to tighten my lips and excuse myself, very carefully, to the ladies room. Where minutes before I was ravenous, suddenly even the smell of food was making me nauseous. Never before did I feel that but then realized I wasn't pregnant before either.

Let the morning sickness commence, I thought with despair.

I dry heaved a bit into a toilet and then almost vomited at even the thought of my head being so close to a public toilet. I stood up, too quickly, but recovered and cleaned myself up to return to the table. I didn't take very long, so I was surprised I was returning to an empty table. "I asked them to take it away. I didn't realize you were pregnant."

Damn! This wouldn't be as easy to hide as I wanted it to be.

"I just found out. I really didn't tell anyone outside of my blog readers."

"Oh my! I'm sorry I missed that one! I would have opted for a walk in the park instead."

"It's okay. I didn't mean to post it so took it down very quickly. Unfortunately, it already had some comments so feel this could become a thing anytime now."

"What if you announced it on my show? We can do a call in, video record it and I'll give you the rights to publish it through YouTube and on your site?"

"I don't know about all that. I haven't even seen a doctor yet."

"Think about it. I'll get my lawyer to draw up a contract that's great for both of us. You can read it over and we'll plan to meet again next week. I already called Ed, he'll be here to pick you up in five minutes. I'll wait outside with you. Fresh air is great for everything."

"What do I leave for my food? I didn't get a bill."

"It's all taken care of. My treat, or rather, my pleasure of meeting you."

We slowly walked outside, still unstable and now even hungrier than before. Lucy was right, the fresh air did me good only now I really wanted that chicken. "Do you have kids?" I dared to ask.

"Two. Both teenagers now and rarely home. It makes me miss babies. You'll be a fine mom."

"You're so young to have teenagers! I don't know how you've been able to stay so fit."

"You're not doing too bad yourself. It impresses me that you started your life again so late. I feel like I'm already half way dead some days."

"Goodness, you hid it well."

"Oh, there's Ed." He parked in front of us and Lucy opened the door and got in after me. "Ed, please take Annabelle home first but, the long way around. Thank you." I noticed she used the button I was pondering about and the window dividing us from the driver raised. "Annabelle, I think you have something great here. In a time where people think they are too busy to drink a glass of water, you're having them stop and read a blog. And comment on it! That is no small feat.

"I started young and still haven't figured everything out but it seems you're making great progress and don't even know what you're doing, no offence. Let me help you never actually work again!"

She handed me her business card after scribbling something on it as we pulled up to Travis's apartment. "That's my direct number, truly, call me anytime about anything."

"Thank you," was all I said. My stomach screaming at me again, like tiny butterflies with many daggers. The possibility of not working again was tempting but I wasn't sure it would ever be possible, especially with a little one on the way. Ed opened my door and I left without saying anything else. My lips so tightly sealed I was afraid it wouldn't be words coming out if I dared loosen them.

Chapter Eighteen

I was surprised to see Travis waiting for me when I stumbled into the apartment and bee-lined for the bathroom. He came in behind me and held my hair back as I stared at my reflection in the toilet water. "So I'm guessing I shouldn't ask how lunch was?"

"Crackers and peanut butter, please," I pushed out of my voice box. "And some water and some orange juice." My throat was dry and raw so my words came out roughly but Travis understood and retreated to the kitchen. I heard him rummaging through cupboards followed by the clinking of glasses and then silence. He returned to the bathroom with a tray filled with a variety of crackers, a jar of peanut butter and a glass of water.

"Out of orange juice and most of these crackers are likely stale. When you feel better I'll run to the store for whatever you need."

"Thank you," I said as I spread peanut butter on a cracker with my finger. "You forgot the knife," I commented through strained laughter. My dry throat made dryer with the saltine as I tried to swallow it down. I chased it with water as Travis disappeared, presumably to get a knife.

Standing up I got dizzy but braved carrying the tray to the couch where I slumped into the corner. Travis sat beside me, handing me a knife and then offered to spread the peanut butter. "No thanks, I got this. I hate to ask, but do you mind going for orange juice? Before you do, I feel a barf bucket might be a good idea."

"As long as you tell me about your meeting with Lucy when I get back."

"Deal," I said and shoved another peanut buttered cracker in my mouth. While Travis was gone I continued to eat, feeling better by the cracker, and repeated Lucy's words over and over again like a mantra. When Travis returned just 30 minutes later, all the crackers were gone including the stale ones and I was still hungry. By the time he poured me a glass of orange juice I smelled his lunch wafting from his empty burger wrapper, and breath, and was jealous. "This pregnancy may end up being the death of me. The smell of your burger is even turning my stomach. I love burgers."

"I ate it on the way to try to avoid this. Kate explained that while this pregnancy stage is different for everyone, avoiding meat and strong smells may be best."

"How is she always so right? I feel hungry, but satisfied. Thanks for running out for more staples. For future, those are always my go to's when I'm not feeling well."

"I'll keep some on hand at all times," Travis promised. "Feel up to telling me about your meeting? Need anything else before you do?"

"I'd love to tell you all about it; I'm fine for food and drinks now, though." After taking a mouthful of orange juice to soothe my throat I told him everything, concluding with the surprising decision I didn't realize I had already made. "I'm going to do it. I think this could be a way for me to both get through my pregnancy and earn a bit of money while I look for a job."

Travis was supportive and excited for me. He also suggested I wait until after the doctor's appointment in the morning to call Lucy back. Just as a precaution and some reassurance that we weren't getting ahead of ourselves. It didn't go unnoticed that he always said "we" and "us" and it warmed me inside. We decided to watch "What To Expect When You're Expecting" and then make a list of questions to ask the doctor the next morning.

We both laughed and cried the entire time, filling our notebooks with numerous questions and equally enjoying the movie and being terrified of it all. It was so hard to be confident and calm while also learning how much having a child would both cost us.

When the movie concluded. Travis turned to me and asked for my first question. I didn't need to look at my paper for this one as it was only for him and trumped all others. "Are you sure you want to do this?"

"Absolutely," he confidently replied without a second of hesitation. It made me feel even more confused as I was doubting myself while he was all in. "Second question?"

"Are you sure you want to do this with me?"

"Absolutely. You are the only person I could ever imagine doing this with and for the rest of my life. My turn. Do you want to do this?"

"I think so? I mean, I never imagined being in this position in all my life. Even as a little girl, I doubted my desires as a mother but, and this is a big but, this seems right somehow. I'm excited as well as terrified, hopeful while being realistic. So many women my age struggle with keeping the baby, with going full term. That and we're not really well off or financially ready, of course quitting my job wasn't great timing."

"We'll figure it out. All we can do is take it one day at a time. I have some interviews lined up next week, you'll do the podcast and get more eyes on your blog increasing your affiliate and advertising opportunities. Look at Kate; alone and starting over in a new city again, but she's getting there."

"I guess you're right. Ok, let's pare down our list for the doctor. We can't overwhelm him in the first appointment and some may not be as important for the first one."

We went through our questions, making a new list with our combined higher priority concerns and, once satisfied we had a good list, we went to bed. We both wanted a good sleep and had to be up early so tried our best to get to sleep quickly. Unfortunately, we were both wide awake and trembling with excitement. Fortunately, we had a wonderful way to release that nervous energy and fell quickly into a deep sleep after some bedroom antics.

Chapter Nineteen

Travis and I both struggled to get out of bed; neither of us ready to face the day. While I showered he made breakfast and I picked at mine while he showered. It wasn't clear if it was the little one inside me causing me to lose my appetite or the idea of it all. It really didn't matter but I did know I had to eat something, so took a few mouthfuls of egg and swallowed them with a glass of orange juice. I then noticed Arrow Root cookies on the counter and grabbed one, shoving the rest of a sleeve in my bag. It was just what my stomach needed and I was impressed with Travis's thoughtfulness.

We drove to the doctor's office in silence and arrived fifteen minutes before our time. We both just sat in the car staring at nothing and holding our breaths. Finally I said, "The receptionist wanted us to come in ten minutes early so we better get in there." A fairly new relationship, I wasn't sure if silence was how Travis dealt with stress or excitement. It did seem uncharacteristic of him, so I made a mental note to ask him about it later. We got out at the same time and met at the door; he held it open for me and then grabbed my hand and squeezed it gently as we approached the front desk. I cleared my throat and squeaked out my name, as if she didn't already know. No one else was in the waiting room.

"Ah yes, here's your file. Welcome back. Come on back," she said with a smile I struggled to return. She handed me a jar and directed me first to the bathroom where I filled the toilet, as well as covered it. I tried to wipe it off as best I could, but it was a mess. I opened the door to see her still standing there, now with a gloved hand, and she took the jar. "Good," she commented though didn't clarify. "I'll just be a moment," she said and disappeared in a back room. Returning just seconds later she commented that the doctor would have the results and join us right away.

"Wow, this is service! I usually have to wait a half an hour before the doctor is even in," Travis noted.

The receptionist barely smiled at him to acknowledge he spoke. I squeezed his hand back.

"Sir, I'll ask that you to sit in the waiting room," the receptionist instructed after guiding me to the room with the dreaded table. It was definitely more an order than a question. I had flash backs of the whole waxing experience and flinched.

"Can he stay? I know it's a small room, but I'd be more comfortable if he stayed."

"The doctor will want to examine you first and talk to you alone, but then you can ask him to come in."

I didn't like that at all, but wasn't going to discuss it with her. I didn't have enough focus or energy to argue with someone who was just following rules and couldn't seem to bend them. Travis went around her, much to her distaste, and hugged me whispering, "I'll be right outside the door." He kissed me and then left the room.

With him gone, the receptionist asked that I undress from the waist down and lay on the table. The room was cold in many ways, but I complied once she left the room and closed the door promising the doctor would be right in. I stared at the ceiling trying to clear my mind as I waited but, she was right, I didn't wait long.

"Anne, how are you?"

"Annabelle now, please. I'm OK. Listen, I know it's not normal, but I'd like my boyfriend and father of my child to be in here. The receptionist said I needed to clear it with you."

He seemed to ponder my request for a moment and finally said he needed to ask me a few questions privately first but then it would be OK. As he started the examination, though I'm not sure what he was looking for as the nugget wouldn't be big enough to see yet, he asked how I was feeling. It took me a minute to realize he meant it as more than small talk and work the courage up to reply. "Morning sickness has started and I only have an appetite for Arrow Root cookies of all things."

As his head was buried under the blanket, I felt my body tense and knew it would be worse if I didn't just ease up. It was at that moment I realized I didn't clean up down there and all the hair was straggly and curly. It must have looked like a jungle down there which didn't help the tension. At one point one of his tools even got caught in a knot and, as he pulled, I yelped a little and bit on my lip.

"All done. Now for a serious question. Do you want this baby?"

It was blunt, like the tools he was using, but also necessary. One of the questions I kept asking myself though never thought I'd have a choice at this point. I couldn't just say – no, give it to someone else. Or just take it out, doc. That wasn't something I could do.

He was waiting for an answer so I gave him the only one I could, "Of course. If he or she will have me. I know there are many factors at play here."

"There are, you're right. We'll talk about that in my office. You're good to put your pants on and I'll meet you in the room across the hall when you're ready. I'll get your boyfriend to join us." He left the room as I thanked him, awkwardly trying to maintain eye contact while still laying on the table with my legs spread. As I sat up he open the door again, thankfully I was still covered with the blanket though he already saw it all, anyway. There wasn't much left to hide.

"Sorry, one more thing before we go into my office. Can you lift up your shirt?"

I hesitantly followed the doctor's orders, unclear of what he'd be checking at this early stage. "Bra, too."

He approached and mumbled an excuse me as he flicked my right nipple with his index finger. At the same time he pinched my left nipple and declared, "You'll have no trouble breastfeeding, I suspect. See you in a minute." He left and closed the door as I adjusted and wondered if that was completely necessary.

I took a deep breath and wiped a few tears before making my way across the hall and into Doctor Nickerson's office. He was behind his desk and Travis sat in front of it. The tension was obvious and there were no words between them. Sitting down beside Travis, he immediately took hold of my hand and squeezed gently. The doctor spoke first and looked only at me.

"I'm going to refer you to get blood work but, I tested your urine and it's confirmed. Annabelle, you are pregnant. Of course, we don't know how far along you are yet, but we'll figure that all out." Travis squeezed my hand tighter and was smiling while my face seemed frozen. "I'll refer you to a gynecologist, Doctor Gee, who will be in contact with you soon. I'm sure you both can appreciate, under these circumstances, how closely we'll need to monitor everything. It would be wise to advise your employer soon, don't bother waiting the three months, as you will need regular check-ups."

More confirmation I was better off working for myself, at least for a little while. "Thank you. We do have some questions, but now I wonder if it's best to wait."

"I am sorry, I don't have much time and Doctor Gee will know much more than I with respect to all of this." He made a point of checking his watch before commenting, "I do have a few minutes, if you have some immediate ones."

Travis started with one that was clearly important to him and, I regretfully admitted, to me, too. "Is intercourse safe for the baby?" I was grateful he asked as he was more casual about it while I would have stupidly been embarrassed to ask.

Thankfully the doctored remained professional despite the look of delight sparkling in his eyes. "Oh yes, nothing in that manner would harm the little one. It might actually be good as it will relax Annabelle and give her a chance to destress."

That settled, I jumped right into the next question, "What about vitamins and exercise? I assume I stop taking my birth control pill." It seemed silly to ask, but was on my mind.

"Oh yes, stop immediately if you haven't already. And start taking multi-vitamins, there is one specifically for pregnant mothers. It has all the right things to help strengthen your chances of a full term pregnancy. Sorry, you must excuse me now," he concluded with another glance at his watch.

"Thank you for your time. I'll leave my number with the receptionist?"

"Yes, and she'll give you some paperwork to get some bloodwork done at the hospital. Congratulations!"

He seemed more personable again by the end of the appointment. Though my regular doctor for many years, even for my bi-annual pap-smear, the nipple flick seemed out of line for him. It still haunted me and stuck in the back of my mind, so I was thankful when he said I'd have to be referred to someone new.

Chapter Twenty

Travis took me out to a lovely brunch before we went home and, while it was only toast with jam and a small apple juice, I was able to finish it all. And the smell of his bacon and eggs didn't bother me a bit. I hoped that a lot of yesterday's nerves were from the doctor's appointment but, with that out of the way, I could relax a bit.

During brunch we talked about the idea of moving to a bigger place, though decided we were getting ahead of ourselves. The two bedroom apartment would accommodate us and a child for a little while and, with his job search just getting started, we didn't want to commit to something before knowing where we'd be.

"To save on expenses, I'll start cleaning out my storage locker and purge a lot of the stuff. I never got around to sorting through it and haven't needed anything from it for years, so I'm sure it can mostly just be thrown out or donated. Feel like helping?"

"Absolutely. More content for my blog," I said with a wink not knowing how right that statement would be.

When we got home we both realized our phones were still on silent and I missed a few calls.

Three from Lucy and one from Doctor Gee's office. I called the doctor back first.

"Sorry, it's Annabelle Tracy. I see I missed your call." I heard the woman rifle through some papers after asking me politely to hold. She came back quickly and started with a "Congratulations!" I know it's short notice but can you come in today at three?"

I whispered three to Travis who nodded as his eyebrows cringed up. I help up a finger to him as I replied into the receiver, "Three sounds good. Anything I need to know beforehand?"

"Just bring yourself and, if you'd like, the father or a friend. Doctor Gee will need to do another more thorough examination when you come in. Did you already get your bloodwork done?"

"Oh shoot, no. Can I just walk in and get it at the clinic?"

"Yes, please do that soon to give them time to get it to us. Doctor Gee is quite concerned about your… circumstances and wants everything done that can be."

"Ok, I'll go in right now. Thanks for calling and we'll see you at three."

I didn't even have my shoes off and noticed Travis was half way before freezing, confused by my half of the conversation. "We, or rather, I need to go to the clinic for bloodwork now and see Doctor Gee at three. You don't need to go if you have other plans."

"I'll cancel them. You are priority now." He put on his other shoe again and grabbed the keys from the hook. "All set?"

"Thank you, Travis. This is all happening so fast which is kind of good, it gives me less time to stress over it."

The closest clinic, located in the hospital, had an hour long wait so we decided to try the next one. It was another ten minutes away, but was private and specialized in blood tests. We only waited ten minutes and were promised the results would be forwarded to Doctor Gee's office by 2 PM.

Looking at the time I realized we had a couple of hours before the appointment so I asked Travis a strange question I never thought I'd ask in my life, "Travis, do you think you could shave me before the appointment?" We were alone, waiting for the nurse to draw my blood, when I asked.

"Umm, I guess so," I wasn't sure if he was just shocked by my question or confused.

"I'm new to shaving, you know, down there, and the doctor will be looking there again. I thought you might have a better angle to clean things up."

"Oh, yes, I mean, it will be my first time, but I would assume it's like shaving my beard." He said that just as the nurse came up behind him and, by the look on her face, she somehow figured out what we were talking about but said nothing.

She drew the blood quickly and easily and rushed away without much conversation. I preferred it that way. Not necessarily scared of needles but not a big fan of small talk while I tried to remain distracted. Instructed to sit for fifteen minutes in the waiting room, we made our way over to an empty seat in a corner while Travis stood leaning against the wall. I held my little square material in place just like the doctor ordered.

We were silent as we looked over the crowd and I spotted a little girl colouring at the table in the middle of the waiting area. She caught me staring and came over, bringing her page in one hand and a doll in the other. "Look what I did," she said proudly as she held up scribbles on her page. I froze, not ever being around kids, and just stared at her.

An adult, presumably her mother, rushed over apologizing on behalf of her daughter who must have been only three or four. She said it at the same time Travis bent down, inspecting the page closer and commenting on the beautiful blue and pink she used for the goldfish. "I think that one should be framed, what do you think, Annabelle?" It seemed like he sensed my anxiety and wanted to include me, while telling the mother it was OK. That we was thankful for the pig-tailed distraction.

The mother remained close by while Travis carried on a very basic conversation with the little girl and finally, learning her name, introduced us. When her name was called our waiting time was up so we said our goodbyes and went our separate ways.

Outside I turned to Travis and commented on his great ability to make friends with everyone, no matter their age. "Do you want a boy or girl," he asked in response.

"Doesn't really matter," I thought but contemplated further. "A girl I think…"

"As long as he or she is healthy, I'm OK with either though a boy would be fun. And I know much more about boys than girls."

"Yes, a boy. That's my choice, too."

"Then again, I raised Katie most of my life and she turned out pretty good, I think."

We both laughed and agreed, a healthy baby would be best. We went home after making a quick pit stop for razors, shaving cream and a quick chat with Megan. We agreed on not sharing the news with her just yet but, she seemed to sense something was up by her giddiness. With a promise to fill her in later, she rang through our purchases and wished us a good day.

Chapter Twenty-One

When we returned home we both had a shower, making my skin more supple and ready for shaving. With our time limited, we simply enjoyed washing each other quickly, with a few intense kisses, and then he laid a towel down on the floor in preparation. Looking at it I realized there wasn't enough room in the bathroom so led him to the living room where I put a blanket down and then two towels to protect the hardwood.

Still completely naked, I laid on my back and spread my legs while he kneeled between them. "Are you sure you want me to do this?"

"I figure you can clean it up better with the optimal view. I have only done it once and am not sure I got it all. So yes, please go ahead."

I felt his thumb navigate between my folds as he squirted shaving cream on the entire area with the other hand. From my perspective it felt like he used the entire can, but I said nothing. It was hard not to squirm as he brought the razor to a lip and began. While my whole body remained damp, I could feel myself moisten and realized it wasn't entirely the shaving cream at fault.

I stayed silent. And still.

Travis seemed to be taking forever, but then squirted even more shaving cream on and was, by that time, laying on his belly and positioning himself for a much closer inspection. It was then I saw the door knob to our apartment turn and, while I tried to convince myself the door was locked, Kate entered. "Oh my!" she gasped as I jerked causing Travis to let go of the razor. I felt it slice just a tiny bit and grimaced while trying to roll the blanket over me. I wasn't one bit graceful in doing so, but finally managed.

Somehow I managed to be face down on the floor but wrapped and covered, realizing too late how much shaving cream must have been rubbed into the towels and blankets. One tiny bit of relief was realizing Travis put on a pair of shorts at least.

Wiggling my way around and into a sitting position wasn't easy but I was finally up, still covered, and facing Kate. "What did I come into? The door wasn't even locked!"

I tried to explain but my tongue was tied with embarrassment and Travis finally took over. I was terrified at the idea of someone knowing I asked him to do this, but the cat was out of the bag, as some would say. I appreciated his ability to remain calm and fill her in.

"Wow, Doctor Gee is one of the best! I had to see him once while my doctor was away. You'll love him. Kudo's to you for the effort in making a great first impression. Maybe if criminology doesn't work out for you, you can find a job at that waxing place, bro."

"Ha-ha! Can you explain why you're here please and then politely make your exit and forget everything you saw here today?"

"Fat chance of that happening. Oof, poor use of words. No, brother, that one is burned deep but damn, Annabelle, the gym and pregnancy is giving you a glow!"

"Uh… thanks… I guess." It didn't seem like a moment of gratitude but I didn't really know what else to say.

"I just came to get my last box of stuff and to give you some money."

"Money?"

"I got my first pay check and wanted to give you something for letting me stay here."

"Don't be an idiot. You're my sister. And I may need to hit you up for a room in the future if I can't find a job. Keep it. You deserve your entire check."

She didn't argue and instead put the cash back in her pocket and escaped to the spare room. "We need to always lock the door, Travis," I whispered from my spot on the floor. "Even though she has a key and could have let herself in."

"Right, and to give you your key." Apparently my vantage point was lacking and she was quieter on her feet than I thought. She tried to hand me the key, but my hands were busy holding the blankets around me so she gave it to Travis instead. "I figured Annabelle would be needing her own and I don't need it anymore. I'll start knocking too, though. I've learned my lesson."

Once she was gone Travis locked the door behind her and looked at the clock on the wall. "We better get going, it's already 2 PM." The shower and shave must have taken a lot longer than it seemed and I stood, letting the blankets fall, and rushed to the bathroom to wipe off any remaining residue. It was then I realized how much that tiny cut stung, but I didn't have time to take a closer inspection. I should have made time to look.

I quickly got dressed and made our way to the doctor's office. Travis remembered the notebook with our questions. When we entered the office it was pretty much the same routine as earlier that day with the receptionist bringing me to a room with the table and asking me to undress from the waist down. "You can leave your socks on," she said with a smile and was out the door.

Before she got it closed I asked her to come back, asked if Travis could come in. The room was bigger, there was a chair in the corner so he'd be out of the doctor's way. "Yes, if you'd prefer. I'll send him in."

Relieved by not having to argue this time and at the idea of having him in, I relaxed a little and got undressed. By the time Travis returned, I was laying back on the table and in position. I figured it was easier to do then versus waiting until the doctor came in, though was also second guessing my choice, especially after seeing Travis face. It was a cross between him holding back a laugh and what appeared to be suppressing mortification, but the doctor came in before I could ask.

"Hi, Annabelle. I'm Doctor Gee. Congratulations. Will this be your first?" He took his position at the end of the table, barely making eye contact with me before seeing my vagina. He didn't even seem to notice Travis sitting there, with his hand over his mouth and appearing to be holding back a bowel movement.

"Yes, it will. For both of us. That's Travis." I was trying to stare at the ceiling, grateful the sheet was covering the doctor's face and mine from his. That was until he looked up from his inspection, looked right at me and, while seemingly holding back laughter, maintained a professional conversation.

Once the doctor excused himself, instructing me to get dressed and promising to be back in a few minutes, I asked Travis what was wrong.

"I'm not sure you want to know," was his reply as he released his laugh quietly. "I sort of missed a spot and the nick I gave you was a little puffy. I'm so sorry. I feel terrible."

He didn't look like he felt terrible, but I hoped in later years I could see the humour in it all. At that time though, I was horrified and not looking forward to seeing Doctor Gee again. Then he was in the same room, like he promised.

Chapter Twenty-Two

It was weird but during the entire appointment, which didn't feel rushed in the slightest, and left us with as many questions as we had answered, Doctor Gee didn't once look at Travis. When Travis asked a question, Doctor Gee could obviously hear him, but waited for me to rephrase it. Travis waited until we were home to bring it up.

"Do you think he's deliberately ignoring me because we're not married?"

I was shocked by his question, hoping he didn't notice and the relationship being too new to even think about marriage. Yet, it did make sense. Neither of us were wearing a ring, I was pregnant and made it clear he was the father, yet the doctor wouldn't even acknowledge his existence. "I'm sure he didn't even notice and, these days, most women he sees likely aren't married. It's just the first appointment, I'm sure he'll warm up to you. Can we just watch a movie and forget about the day? Not that forgetting is something we should or can do at this point. I'm in the mood for popcorn and Jim Carey."

"Classic or a new one?"

"How about Yes Man?"

Travis prepared the popcorn as I changed into my favourite pajamas after first getting a mirror. Taking off my panties and positioning the mirror to see the mess below I cringed. The tiny cut was making a big scene and the tuft of hair in the back reminded me of one of those tiny mustaches, just under the nose. I grabbed the razor and at least got rid of that before dressing.

Returning to the living room I was delighted to see a bowl of popcorn, line up of flavouring and a glass of ginger ale on the table with a blanket on the couch. "Maybe we should clean that first," I mentioned, recalling the mess I made.

"It's the one that was on the bottom, it's clean. The others are in the washer, I'll get this one cleaned tomorrow. I'll be right back. Get comfy."

He didn't have to tell me twice. I curled up under the blanket and found Yes Man, pausing it so we could watch it together from the very beginning. Travis returned dressed in pajama pants, a hoodie and dog slippers I was seeing for the first time. He noticed me noticing and asked if I was jealous.

I laughed in response and immediately felt bad about it.

"I was obsessed with dogs as a kid. Not just any dog, either. Bull Mastiff's. Kate got me these for Christmas many years ago, the closest to a Mastiff she could find. They may be ratty but they are my favourite movie watching slippers I have."

"Oh, so I should prepare myself for a line of men's slippers, huh?" I teased but was also very curious what other surprises he had in store for me.

As he sat down I leaned over to give him a peck on the cheek and snuggled into him as I started the movie.

We fed each other enough popcorn to make an elephant happy and fell asleep satisfied and in good spirits. When we woke up the next morning by the sound of a knock at the door, we realized we had absolutely no plans for the day and expected no company.

My body creaked as I stood up from the couch, reminding me just how old I was despite all efforts and activities to stay young, and I answered the door.

"Sorry to wake you, I just need your signature," the stranger holding a registered letter said.

"Oh, it must be for you, Travis," I turned away from the man and invited Travis to sign.

"Actually, no, it's for an Annabelle Gray. This is apartment 3C, yes?"

"Oh, yes, sorry, I'm Annabelle. I'll sign."

I opened the envelope after closing, and locking the door and gasped. It was the offer from Lucy and seemed like a considerable amount from a Pod Cast operation. Travis stood behind me, wrapped his arms around my waist as he looked over my shoulder to see what I was looking at.

"What are you going to do?"

"I don't really know. Advice? It seems like too nice of a chunk of change to have to turn it down but, I don't know if I'm ready to go so public."

"Let's take a day to read it and think it through. I was going to start cleaning out my storage locker and would love for you to join me. After graduation tomorrow I'm going to have to start interviewing for jobs so may not have a day off for a while. If you'll join me, we can chat it through and decide what to do. Of course, the decision is entirely yours, but I'm here to talk it out. It's not all about the money, I have some saved up and we'll figure out something."

"Thanks, Travis. That sounds like a great day to me and I cannot wait to see what you've been storing. I'm hoping for baby pictures and old toys so I can learn more about you."

"I'm sure you'll come to find out that I'm a pretty boring guy. Sounds like a plan, though. I'll list most for sale, keep some and trash others. Who was it that said if it didn't bring you joy get rid of it? Well, my joy barometer has changed since meeting you."

"Marie Kondo. I read all of her books, hence, I really have nothing to my name, but feel joyous about it."

We ate breakfast together, each taking a turn to read through the contract without comment. It was hard not to react, but we somehow both managed. I had no idea what Travis was thinking and barely knew what I was thinking. It was scary to think anyone would care about me enough to tune in but, Lucy was right, people were flocking to my website already and that was just journal entries really. Turns out, the figure was an annual salary to be a co-host, not just a one-time guest. A job with the flexibility of working from home and when I wanted, without having to take away from my own blog.

After we showered, dressed and packed a lunch to eat at the storage locker, I put the contract in my purse as well as a notepad. The weather was great so we walked to the locker, chatting about what book we would read together next. Having finished Arm Farm long ago and knowing we needed to find time to relax, the list was endless as we both loved the same genre. Keeping it light helped reduce my nerves about all the heavy stuff we've been dealing with lately so I was thankful.

Once we arrived and decided on a game plan, I found a box suitable to sit on and Travis moved one close to me, inviting me to open it. The side had "BLANKETS" written on it, but he said that really didn't mean anything. He went to the other side of the locker, not four feet away, and did the same. "One, two, three… open," he announced.

Looking into mine I saw, not surprisingly, a nice wool blanket the colour of the ocean on a sunny day. I felt its softness and realized someone special to him must have made it. I brought it to my nose and instantly regretted it. While there were soft undertones of the sweetness that comes with old blankets, the most fragrant layer was dust from being packed away.

"Aww… That's a definite keep, though a must wash. It was the only thing left to me by my mother. I like to think that her mother or grandmother made it and passed it along the generations. I'll pass it along to our little one." He was holding a bundle of comic books that looked in pristine condition. I set the blanket aside and looked inside the box, not being able to hide my surprise. As I held it up Travis stood and said, "Let me explain!"

Chapter Twenty-Three

The plastic unfolded revealing a face with a mouth in the same shape as my own – a circle. Its lips painted a bright red and its eyes a light blue. Brown hair was painted on the top in the shape of a pony tail. It was stuck together but as I held it up, reaching above my head, it unfurled and revealed a quite endowed image of a woman. "Your ex-girlfriend?"

Travis was clearly nervous and, for the first time since I have known him, speechless. I realized he must not have remembered having it at all, or at least that he stored it in this box under his cherished blanket, or else I wouldn't have been the one to find it. Our relationship was still fairly new, I understood, and we didn't talk much about our past relationships, but I was still shocked and undecided about how to feel otherwise about this find.

"This really isn't what I was expecting to find out about your past today. I envisioned dolls but more G.I. Joe's and action figures; well, I guess this could be considered an action figure. Just… no need to explain. Keep, sell or throw out. Tell me, Travis. Does Betsy bring you joy?" I was trying to be kind, but was also a bit disgusted and not hiding it well. I was feeling many things and wasn't quite sure what to settle on yet.

By this time Travis was standing beside me and taking the doll by an arm. I let go and he moved to shove it back in the box. It made me wonder what else was in there under the next blanket but I decided I wasn't ready for that. It seemed he wasn't either, as he moved it away from me and replaced it with another box.

"Do you want to talk about that now or later?" At least he was offering to discuss it and not simply hide it away.

"I think now might be a good time," though I wasn't really convinced. "I'll try not to judge but, if you don't want to talk about it now we can do it later. I'll just warn you that in the meantime my imagination might make it out to be worse than it is."

"It was a friends."

"Please don't lie. I do much better with whatever harsh truth is behind this than any lie you're going to try to make me believe."

"No, really. Well, it was a friends. Stewart, you haven't met him yet but will, he's a good guy with great intentions." Travis moved back to his seat and I opened the replacement box as he spoke. "He kept himself busy with school, work, looking after his siblings too much while his mother got sick. He had absolutely no time for a girlfriend. He was just turning twenty, all his mates were finding partners and he was just so tired of life. It was really a sad situation, but he was excelling, just burning out at the same time.

"A friend, not me, tried to suggest weed and another recommended harder drugs to help him relax, but he was dead set against them. His father went to jail for dealing and Stewart vowed to never touch even an Advil unless he was desperate. Then one night he watched this show Dummy and wanted to see if a plastic companion would help. He didn't think it through. He was on such little sleep, his mind was lost. No way could he hide a doll in his house and not have one of the kids come across it.

"He ordered it in an absolute stupor and was surprised when it arrived. Thankfully I remembered the conversation and was with him when it was left on the doorstep. I was able to convince him not to open it in front of his family and to leave it in his room. It was hilarious to have him not know what it was and the packaging was indiscrete, of course."

"What did you do?"

"Well, he shared his room with his little brother so we put it in his closet to start, but then I took it when I went home. He came over after and we tried to figure out a way to make it work, but couldn't. He wouldn't take it home so left it at my place since I lived alone at that time."

"Dare I ask if he had to use it at your place, too?"

"That's the thing. He moved away shortly after and I was stuck with… her… I shoved her away and never thought of it again until now."

"So… throw out?" I didn't want to press too hard and I did believe his story, it sounded too detailed to just be made up but, something was still off.

"I'm certainly not going to sell it," he replied and I left it at that. We continued going through other mundane things, enlarging the sell and throw out piles much faster than the to-keep pile. I tried not to worry about it but, couldn't get it off my mind and kept glancing towards the box.

My opportunity came when his phone rang and he answered it, excused himself and was speaking more professionally than usual. I took out my phone, not wanting to go through his things without his presence. Once I could no longer hear him, however, I poked my head out the door to confirm he was far enough away and returned to the mystery box. I moved the next blanket cautiously, not wanting to leave evidence of my snooping, and gasped when I saw some things I barely recognized. Items of all colours and shapes, lotions, and condoms. This wasn't his blanket box, this was his treasure box!

I sensed his return more than heard it and instantly felt guilty. "I'm sorry, I couldn't resist. It's OK. You don't need to explain. We both have our histories we haven't shared yet. Apparently yours was just feistier than mine."

He kissed me. I wasn't sure if he heard me or didn't, knew what I saw or not, but the kiss was promising, eager and welcome. After such an interesting day this was inviting.

"I got an interview!"

"Oh my gosh, already? When? For where?"

"Right here in the city. At the school, actually. Teaching the class. Apparently my professor is retiring and they need a replacement quickly. They said I could then choose to take courses for free to get my teacher's license, while I work, and keep the job permanently or just fill in temporarily until they find a permanent replacement. The interview is more of a formality but, it sounds promising."

I squeezed his hands and kissed him again. "Congratulations, Travis! You would make an awesome teacher. What are you going to do?"

"Well, I'll go for the interview and see what they offer but, it sounds like it would be a good way to start my career. I'm not sure about teaching permanently, however. I think I'd want to be more hands on, in the field."

"Don't sacrifice what you want from life for me."

"I don't need anything but you, Annabelle but I hear you."

Chapter Twenty-Four

Between doctor visits, interviews and my decision to do the podcast, at least temporarily, life kept us busy and it took a month to clean out the storage locker. There were no more shocking discoveries that I opened, but the blanket box still sat in the corner as many other things were sold or waiting to sell.

"I say we just donate the rest. They aren't selling and I'm not paying to store them any longer."

"I think that's very wise of you. If you want, I can take them to Value Village tomorrow. Megan and I were trying to find a reason to go there anyway."

"Sure! Do you think she can pick them up to put in her van? I'll give you the key so you can just come back tomorrow. Or would you rather get a hold of her tonight and I can help load? I don't want you to lift a finger."

"Let me call her now." I excused myself from the depths of the locker so I could get better reception. She agreed to come in the morning and said she'd be fine lifting everything. Promising to not let me lift a finger, though she didn't yet know why, and to take the items out of the boxes if one was too heavy for me. I returned to the locker to see Travis staring at the box with the blankets and other items.

"All set for morning. She says she'll be fine and knows not to let me lift a finger." He remained still, as if he didn't hear me, so I approached quietly and gently rested my hand on my shoulder, trying to see what caught his attention. I gasped when I saw him holding a framed picture whose subject matter was clearly him and his sister at a very young age with an unknown adult between them.

A tear drop landed on the glass and I stayed silent. Waiting until he spoke, I hugged him from behind and stared at the photograph with him. It took him several minutes to speak, but I was happy to wait.

"I forgot we had this. I'm so glad I went through the box again." Looking into the box I noticed he rearranged all the condoms, long expired, and gels and I decided that the toys, that wild part of his history, didn't matter so much anymore.

"Who is that in the middle?" I was gentle, encouraging him to open up a bit more. We had talked a lot the past month but more about our futures than our pasts. "I immediately recognize you and Kate, of course."

"Our grandmother. She hated having her picture taken so these treasures are so rare. The few we had were lost in the shuffling but this one; Kate always had it on her nightstand. I'm not sure why I ended up with it but am so glad I did."

"She looks like she was so kind and strong. You must take after her."

The phone rang then. His phone. We were both startled from this special moment but, it was quickly made more special by the reason for the call. "Travis? I'm on my way to St Vincent's. You're going to be an uncle!"

"We'll be there soon. Yes, Annabelle is with me. We'll be there as soon as we can."

He rushed out of the locker, closing it and then went back in to grab the photo. "She needs it for her nightstand. She needs this more than I do."

"I think that's a grand idea. I'm going to call Megan and cancel tomorrow."

"No, don't. You've been looking forward to this. Hopefully all will go well with Kate and she'll need rest tomorrow. She'll be in good hands and will likely just want to be alone."

"We'll see. I'll text Megan to let her know so she's not surprised if I do have to cancel last minute."

"Should I stop and get her a coffee?"

"Megan?"

"No, Kate. She loves a hot drink and might need the caffeine. What do I bring? Flowers?"

"Travis, take a breath. I'll drive." It was sweet to see him so excited and I could only imagine what he'd be like when he got the call about me. "You go to her room, give her the photo, I'll stop at the gift shop in the hospital and find her something from us both."

He was in such a stupor he just nodded, visibly jittery like he was on his eighth cup of coffee when he hadn't even had one.

We arrived and went our separate ways. I headed into the gift shop until I saw Travis get on the elevator and then went back out of the hospital. I needed a minute to take this all in. Being in that hospital was hard enough, being where my parents recovered from their accident, but more than that, I was out of place. I wasn't Kate's or Travis's family. I barely knew them, if I was being honest. I had no idea if she would want me in the room and didn't know if I wanted to be in the room. Seeing my future, while understanding it could be completely different, was terrifying.

Taking a few deep breaths, I realized this day was not about me in the slightest. I would go into the room if Kate wanted me there. I'd wait outside the door or go home if she wished. I was twice their age and realized I was acting less than half their age. Kate was the one who had the right to be scared, not me. Not yet.

After a few more deep breaths I returned to the gift shop, found a few adorable items, and made my way up to the delivery ward. Rushing out of the elevator and barely being able to see beyond the balloons – green, gender neutral – I bumped into Doctor Gee and said hello.

"Annabelle! Great to see you. Are you ok?"

"Oh yes, just here for a friends delivery. Kate…? Do you know what room she's in?" I realized as soon as I asked that doctor's really wouldn't know anything so trivial so was shocked when he replied. I also was concerned I didn't know her last name. Travis's was Struthers, of course, but was Kate's the same?

"Room seven, I'm heading there now."

"Oh! Are you her doctor?"

"I am today. Doctor Winston is out today so I'm the doctor in charge." We walked quickly as we talked. It took my mind off what we would be walking into so I was grateful.

Entering the room I saw several nurses buzzing about, Travis standing beside Kate who was laying on the bed and he was holding her hand. Kate was dressed in the standard hospital gown and sweating though the room was chilled. I approached hesitantly while a nurse came over and directed me where to put the gifts so they weren't in the way. "Annabelle, thank you! I wasn't sure you'd come."

"I can leave," was a rude reply but there it was.

"No, please stay. I need you both."

Doctor Gee approached looking from Kate, to Travis, to me and through the cycle again. I realized how awful it looked, assuming Doctor Gee remembered Travis from my appointment. I quickly exclaimed:

"Travis isn't the father!"

Chapter Twenty-Five

The room was quickly deprived of oxygen as everyone seemed to gasp at one. Each seemed to misunderstand what I said in a different way. Kate laughed, Travis looked sick, and Doctor Gee looked even more confused.

"Sorry, I… Travis is the father to my baby. Travis is the sister to Kate. Travis is not Kate's baby daddy." I was nervous, I was rambling and not using educated words but it all seemed to ease the tension in the room. Some of it, anyway.

Doctor Gee went on like I wasn't even there, like Travis wasn't still awkwardly holding his sister's hand. "Kate, I'm Doctor Gee. Doctor Winston is out today so you're stuck with me. This is Nurse…" he motioned to a male nurse standing at his side with a clipboard in his hand.

"I'm Nurse Robbins. You let me know what you need and I'll make sure it happens."

"Thank you," Kate said meekly through clenched teeth.

"Please let me know if you expect any other visitors today. Anyone you want in or not allowed in the room, we need to know."

"These are the two. No one else."

Doctor Gee rolled up a stool and looked between Kate's legs as we talked with the nurse. No one tried to bring attention to him, but it was all so very weird to be in the room while this was happening.

"It will be a while yet," Doctor Gee declared as his arm stayed under the sheet while his head raised and he looked right at Kate. "Baby seems to be in position but comfortable there." Turning to Nurse Robbins he said, "Page me when her water breaks."

Kate grunted loudly and the nurses began to scramble. One watched her monitor, another hooked something up to her belly and one went to listen to her heart. Travis and I moved out of the way and pushed ourselves against the wall, trying to make ourselves as small as possible. Travis turned to me and nodded, I turned to see Doctor Gee throw a glove at a trash bin as he walked out the door. The glove missed so Travis crept over and put it in before realizing where the glove just was. We both visibly shuddered.

Kate let out another yelp and then the nurses seemed like someone kicked a bee hive and Kate was the hive. We heard a voice call for Doctor Gee to room seven while a nurse grabbed a cell phone, the others all huddled around Kate's bed doing whatever it is they were doing. Finally the anticipation was explained when Doctor Gee entered the room, "Water broke, huh?"

I felt relieved, always worried something wrong was going to happen but water breaking was normal and explained the hype. Travis took one of

Kate's hands, squeezing himself into as small a space as possible and I went around the bed, making a very large U-shape to get around to her other side and avoid the chaos. The baby was coming.

As Kate's cheerleaders, we helped and encouraged her to push. I ran out a few times to get the very soon to be momma ice chips while Travis rubbed her lips with balm from her hospital bag.

It took a matter of several hours before Travis was asked to cut the cord as the little girl was placed on her momma's chest. Kate nodded, though distracted by her beautiful creation, and Travis took the scissors and cut exactly where the doctor showed him. They then rushed her away, promising Kate a quick return, and the nurses did their things while Doctor Gee resumed position and sutured his patient. "Six pounds, three ounces and eighteen inches long," Doctor Gee declared after a nurse held up a sheet in front of him. "We'll need to do some more testing, but she'll be back in the room soon." The doctor stood, motioning for Nurse Robbins to take over and he did.

Travis and I remained frozen, holding Kate's respective hands and it was obvious neither of us knew where to look or what to say. Finally Kate seemed to fall asleep and her tight grip on my hand was loosening. I was grateful as I could barely feel my fingers.

Slowly releasing my hand from hers I walked to Travis, curious to know how someone could just fall asleep after that ordeal and with all the hustle still happening in the room.

"I'm going to go grab a coffee, want one?" I whispered and was surprised when Kate replied, "Desperately."

I looked to Travis and then to Kate who still had her eyes closed. "Is she OK to have coffee?" Travis shrugged but a hovering nurse said it was fine and recommended the nearby café instead of the cafeteria. "She'll want a good one."

"OK, Kate. I'm going to go and get you a coffee. Your usual?" I turned to the nurse and whispered, "Caffeine and sugar OK?"

They both replied yes to my separate, and very different, questions. I kissed Travis on the cheek and promised I'd return as soon as possible.

Once outside of the hospital, tears sprang from my eyes I didn't even realize I was holding back. What an emotional rollercoaster all of this was and it wasn't even my experience. Well, it was I guess, but the actual ride was being enjoyed by Kate. At least for now. At least it looked like she was enjoying it. That was until this day but that would change.

I sat on the bench outside of the café, not even realizing I walked there already until I smelled the sugary sweetness of delectable drinks. I wiped my face, in hopes there were no lingering tears and went in to order the drinks. I stood to the side, awaiting my order and scanning my social media when I heard my name called, sort of.

"Anne, running errands for your boss? You're more than welcome to come back and work for me. Or with me. Or live with me and not work at all."

I recognized the voice before even looking up, hesitating at first at the use of my abbreviated name and then cringing at the words.

"Chuck."

"Annabelle?" The barista called out. I turned and picked up the tray of drinks, putting my phone back in my back pocket and thanked her.

"Have a good day," I said curtly to Chuck and walked out of the café thankful to notice he was next in line to order. Cringing again when I didn't hear him place his order, but instead heard him walking behind me.

"Hold up!"

Chapter Twenty-Six

"Chuck, we're through. I am in a hurry."
"Your boss can wait. She'll still appreciate you or else she's ridiculous. Come back. We're struggling without you. I'm nothing without you."

I stopped and turned so I was side on, my belly should have been obvious to him yet he kept rambling on about how the company was going to fail if I didn't come back. How he loved me and needed me in his arms.

"Chuck, that is never going to happen. We're through. I've moved on. You should, too. You were fine with the company before I got the promotion. Grow up and leave me alone."

He reached out to me, then. Careful not to upset the drinks, he brushed his hand on my belly and I flinched, nearly spilling them anyway. The look on his face showed disgust and confusion. "Are you not taking care of yourself anymore? What happened to the gym?"

"And that is why we're through. You are so oblivious and rude. Read the room, or listen to me speak. I am three months pregnant, you idiot." And then I realized my mistake. I shouldn't have said how far along I was. Three months ago meant there was a possibility it was Chuck's. Slight but not impossible. It looked to me like he was doing the math so I turned back and started walking away at a faster pace than I should have.

"Wait! Is it mine? How dare you keep this from me." He caught up to me then, grabbed me by the shoulder with such force I dropped the tray of hot drinks. Fortunately some splashed onto his fancy white shoes and light beige pants. It was worth having to pay for more drinks even though I worried my account was empty.

The scene caused enough of a commotion to stop passersby in their tracks and a lady asked if I was alright. "Yes, he's a jerk but one I can handle. Thank you."

She seemed hesitant to leave, but I reassured her and then decided to walk with her as I was needing to go back in that direction anyway. "Actually, hold up." I folded the tray into the nearby garbage, followed by the now empty coffee cups and hustled towards her. "Where did you get that jacket? It's such a pretty colour."

Looking back I saw Chuck had moved on, walking across the street to his awaiting car. It was only a block from the office, but he couldn't be bothered to walk. He could easily cut costs and leave the car parked but that would bruise his ego. I was so glad I discovered the true Chuck before too long. Running into him again confirmed that, though had me worried all over again at the possibility of having his child. I tried to refuse to think of that possibility but it was there all the same.

The lady was talking but I was rudely not registering a word she said. "Apologies and appreciation. I dated him not long ago and he's a bit obsessive. I do love your jacket, but admit to not hearing a word you just said."

"I realized that a few sentences in so have just been practicing my monologue."

"Monologue? Are you an actress?"

"On my way to an audition now. I hope to be one, someday soon."

We were back at the café and I offered to buy her a drink for her assistance. "There's no need but if you insist I won't refuse."

"I do insist. Come on," opening the door and letting her in first. I hoped she didn't want too much and I decided, to save on the cost, to skip mine. I placed my order for Travis and Kate, adding the stranger's small black coffee. The barista remembered me, was surprised I returned so quickly and, added my own drink to the order free of charge saying she recognized something must have gone terribly wrong. I thanked her, so grateful for her kindness, and turned to hand the stranger her drink.

In exchange the stranger gave me her card with the name Shelley on the front. No last name, which I found unusual, but didn't say so. I took it, sliding it into my back pocket and told her to break a leg. While others patrons of the café gave us a weird look at such an unkind thing to say, Shelley laughed and said thanks. We parted ways with smiles on our faces, happy to have met a new friend and have a delicious drink to look forward to. I quickly turned and shouted, "Please let me know how it goes," before realizing I had her number but she didn't have mine. I'd have to text her.

I made my way back to Kate's hospital room, delighted to see her asleep and her little one in Travis arms, both dozing in a chair. I walked in quietly though am not sure why. With all the noise and chaos from the ward I likely wouldn't have been heard if I had high heels on. I set the drinks beside their respective owners and found a place to sit to enjoy my own. I watched Travis only slightly acknowledge my arrival as he stared between long blinks at his beautiful niece.

"Thank you," I heard Kate whisper. I turned to face her, it taking a second before I realized she her gratitude was directed towards me.

"For what?"

"Making Travis happy. For being here."

"I appreciate you having me. I know we're not close and haven't known each other long, but I also feel like I've known you forever."

Travis stirred as did the precious baby. "Wakey, wakey sleepy heads," Kate called as she adjusted herself in the bed and took her first drink. "Give her back."

Travis stood and delivered his perfect little package to Kate. She held her against her breast and the baby started to suckle. I couldn't look away despite the awkwardness. It was such a naturally beautiful sight.

"Does she have a name yet?"

"Candice Sue but I plan to call her Candy."

"That's amazingly sweet and fitting."

"Susan was our mother's name," Travis explained. "And our grandmother always had candy for us when we were able to visit. It's an homage with a twist."

"I love it! Your mother and grandmother would be so very proud."

A nurse came in then to check her, the baby and have them moved out of the delivery room to a ward. "Only one visitor will be allowed today, though."

That was my cue to leave, so I wished them well and promised I'd be back the next day.

"Visiting will be from two to four," the nurse instructed automatically as she fidgeted with one machine or another. I acknowledged her with a nod she may not have seen and darted around her to give Kate, Candy and Travis a kiss all appropriately on different areas of the face.

"See you at home, Travis," I called as I made my way back out of the hospital.

Chapter Twenty-Seven

Over the last few months, the biggest trial of our relationship was that Travis taught me how to drive well enough to get my license. It tested our patience, I almost broke the car a few times and was thankful he at least had an automatic. For a few weeks I contemplated taking the drivers course though hated the idea of being so old in a classroom filled with teenagers.

Thankfully, Travis was persistent, encouraging and talked a lot of sense into me. It did finally make sense, especially with a baby on the way and offering to watch Candy, that I had reliable transportation. I just didn't know if I would ever have the confidence to drive alone. It was nice to have someone in the passenger seat to talk to and distract me, alleviate some of the anxiety I associated with driving. He even taught me to parallel park despite my constant complaints.

Being without a license, and a car, for so long I often forgot that I drove and just automatically take the bus home. The first time I dropped Travis off at school it took me thirty minutes to brave the five minute drive to the mall. The man's voice who took me for my test kept yelling in my head that I didn't have to white knuckle it. He encouraged me to let go of the wheel even a little bit and relax while I sang Carrie Underwood's "Jesus Take the Wheel" song over and over in my head.

Once I parked at the mall I finally let go of the wheel and let out my breath, thankful I found a drive-through spot. I had to walk further than I wanted to though felt it best to ensure the car wasn't damaged.

After only spending forty minutes or so in the mall, I completely forgot that I took the car and stood waiting in line for the next bus. It was automatic, I knew exactly which bus to take and, in my absent mindedness, even expected to see Mike driving. Climbing the stairs and seeing the female driver, I was relieved and took a seat near the back of the bus.

It was too late in the ride to bother getting off early when I finally remembered I took the car. I was digging out the apartment keys and realized they were attached to Travis's car keys. Then I contemplated staying on the bus for a round trip or if it would make more sense to get off. It took nearly the whole day for me to get the car back, after not remembering where I even parked it after I got back to the mall, and then get Travis.

I decided not to share my adventures with him.

So when I exited the hospital, exhausted and excited, I started looking for the car keys again before realizing this time I actually did need to take the bus. Travis would take the car home later.

When I climbed the stairs and looked up I gasped, this time I didn't expect to see Mike but there he was. Trying to keep my head down so he didn't recognize it was me, I failed miserably.

He insisted I sit up front, like old times, and chat with him. He apologized for his actions and actually sounded sincere. I felt a bit more at ease seeing the bus was almost full so sat and chatted. Apparently he was out on bail before his trial. He begged for my forgiveness, asking me to drop all charges and tried to convince me he was sober again. The whole thing was a wakeup call and he was back on track.

I acted like I believed him, that I was going to forgive him and even said the words in hopes he would believe them. I also remembered the legal document I signed for just the day before summoning me to court. I cleared my schedule for it. Ensuring I would not make a doctor's appointment on that day.

And then I realized if he looked closely enough he would see my protruding belly. Thankful I was wearing a baggy shirt, I took more effort into ensuring he didn't notice. I failed miserably as my actions made it more obvious and he finally commented.

"Is it mine?"

I laughed. We didn't have sex, thankfully. It couldn't be his, of that I was certain. He didn't take too kindly at me laughing at him and I saw the rage again. I was blinded by lust the first time we met, I wouldn't be so naïve this time. I pulled the cord to indicate it was my stop. I didn't even know where we were, but convinced him I was meeting a friend close by. I was relieved when he let me off without much protest and it was then I made a vow to avoid the bus and get over my fear of driving.

After the bus pulled away I took a look at my surroundings and was grateful I was in walking distance from Travis's apartment. Despite me living there for weeks by then, I still wasn't comfortable with calling it my home. The walk allowed me to clear my head and feel less guilty about skipping the gym so often, lying to Mike and built my confidence in sharing the experience with Travis.

Chapter Twenty-Eight

I waited until I was home to text Travis for permission to share the news of his niece with Megan. He said Kate gave her approval and hoped I'd bring her by to visit. Then I texted Megan, asking if she could call me, not wanting to call her directly in case she was busy at work. She wrote right back saying to give her a few minutes.

It wasn't until I started getting undressed that I remembered Shelley's card in my back pocket. I fished it out and put it on the night stand while I finished putting on more comfortable clothes. I texted her on my way to the kitchen in hopes of finding something quick and easy to make for dinner. I started boiling water for pasta when my cell phone rang. "Hello?" I answered, not taking a moment to see who it was, assuming it must have been Megan or Shelley. It was neither.

"Annabelle, Lucy here. I wanted to ensure you received my offer."

"Lucy, hey, yes. How generous. You know those gift cards and coupons will do me a great deal of good. I just don't know yet." I did know yet, for some reason or another, hesitated in committing, even to a few guest spots on her show.

"No hurry, well, no big rush but I'm eager to host you. I think it will be great for you and your readers. I hope you're doing well. I won't keep you but please keep me in mind."

I had already decided to do the show, I just wasn't sure when I would be available nor for how long. When I hung up with her I saw that I had a missed call from Megan and a text from Shelley. Shelley got the part! It was such an exciting day for so many.

I called Megan back and told her the news about Kate and Candy. She squealed back with excitement, explaining she just loved babies and was eager to meet her.

"Actually, why don't we visit her tomorrow after dropping off that stuff to Value Village? Visiting hours start at two so I figured if we get out in the morning that'll give us plenty of time to drop off Travis's stuff, look around and get there for visiting hours."

"Awesome! Looking forward to it. I can be ready at 9 AM if you want me to treat you to breakfast. I think it only opens at 10:30 AM so that gives us time for breakfast, loading and then drop off."

"Sounds great to me," I agreed as I added some pasta to the boiling water and stirred. "I'll pick you up then."

Once the pasta was cooked, I drained the pot and added some shredded cheese and sauce. While it warmed, I stirred and called Shelley to congratulate her.

A man answered and I was distracted enough not to realize who it was at first. And then when I heard him call for Shelley I realized. "Chuck?"

"Long time no chat, Annabelle."

My head was spinning, my blood boiling like the pasta water just was and I hung up. Throwing the phone on the counter I tried to figure out how that happened. Shelley didn't seem to know him when she stopped me in the street. They couldn't have gotten that close already.

My phone rang and I saw that it was her number. I let it go to voicemail.

"Annabelle, that was rude. I was simply trying to connect with you to give Shelley her phone back."

I listened to it, several times, before making any sense of it. Once I did I heard the door open, Travis was home. Unfortunately the pasta burned a little in my stupor but I managed to serve enough of the non-burnt supper to fill us both. I added some toast with garlic butter along with a bottle of wine to wash it down with and it turned into a great meal. His excitement and chatter even made me forget about Chuck and Shelley for a minute.

It wasn't until he excused himself to the bathroom that it all came crashing back. I asked him about it once he was back in the kitchen again, drying dishes as quickly as I washed them. His voice of reason convinced me that it was possible Shelley dropped her phone and he picked it up.

"Then why send the text about getting the part?"

"It's Chuck. Who knows with him."

He was right, like usual, so I called Shelley's number again. This time Shelley answered but I did hear Chuck in the background.

"Shelley? It's Annabelle. Are you with Chuck?"

"I am, but it's not what you think. I'm just picking up my phone from him. I must have dropped it in the confusion and I'm repaying him with a coffee."

"Be careful. He's a terrible man."

"Thanks for the warning. And thanks for calling. I wanted to let you know I got the part and realized, too late, that I didn't get your number."

We talked a few more minutes, making plans for a coffee date in the near future and I hung up. The feeling in my stomach was unsettling and had nothing to do with the pregnancy. I truly hoped Shelley would listen to me and stay away, but also knew I was a stranger and Chuck could be convincing.

Travis and I turned in for the night, both having an exciting day ahead of us with his interview and my morning with Megan. We promised to meet at the hospital at 2 PM but also to keep in touch throughout the morning.

Having to pee one last time, my bladder already feeling three times smaller than I was used to, I wiped and was startled to see blood on the toilet paper.

Chapter Twenty-Nine

I gasped but tried to do so quietly as to not bring attention to it. Doctor Gee did mention the possibility of spotting and that I should only be concerned if it was a lot or very often. Being the first sign of anything, I cleaned it up, added a pad to my underwear and decided not to mention it to Travis. Fingers crossed he was not in the mood tonight with all the excitement of the day behind us and the one ahead of us.

Who did I think I was kidding? This kid was always in the mood, but I was able to gently push him away without bringing any unneeded attention to my extra padding when his hand ventured up my shirt. I don't know if it was because I was deprived of touch for so long or if Travis's fingers were really magical, but it was damn hard to reject him. It helped being pregnant, however, as I could just say I was extra tired and he, ever the gentleman, would let me sleep.

We snuggled into each other and he rested one arm around my waist. We were both asleep within minutes despite his snoring and my worry.

The alarm sounded in what seemed like minutes but was hours. I got up in a hurry, eager for the day and to check on the status of my pad. Travis hit the snooze button so I told him I'd shower first and get him up when I was done. I grabbed some clothes and escaped to the bathroom, locking the door behind me which was unusual. I already had an excuse at the ready in case he asked, was thankful I didn't need it.

Inspecting my pad while I urinated, I was relieved that there was just a tiny bit of blood on it. Enough to convince me to wear another to put my mind at ease while away all day, but not enough to make me concerned. I was glad I didn't mention it to Travis the night before while also worrying he'd find my old pad. I put it in my pajama's pocket and was careful with how I carried it out when I was done in the bathroom.

Thankfully, Travis was still in bed and oblivious to my stress level as well as my having locked the door. I leaned over, with freshly brushed teeth and kissed him awake after putting my laundry under the bed where my pillow was. I would deal with that once he was in the shower.

I quickly regretted my decision as I noticed Travis was at the ready when he gently pulled me into bed. "You're going to be late," I whispered between kisses, but then my hand seemed to have a mind of its own as it made its way to his now throbbing penis. I could start his morning off right even if I couldn't invite him in.

Once finished I washed my hands in the bathroom as he showered. I closed the door behind me and quickly disposed of my garbage, hiding it in a cereal box already in the garbage in the kitchen. I made Travis breakfast and wished him luck once he got out of the bathroom. I was all ready to leave, with my shoes and jacket on, before I realized he might want the car for his interview. I was still nervous about driving so took every chance I could to give up the car.

"No, I'll take a cab. Or Kate's car. Actually, I'll take the bus to get Kate's car. She gave me the keys yesterday so I can look in on her apartment. I plan to get a few things for her place, too."

"Perfect. Best of luck again. They will be crazy not to hire you."

"We'll see," he replied as I grabbed the car keys and was on my way.

Megan was waiting outside with a huge smile on her face. My first thought was that she did get lucky that morning and I giggled. She hurried to the car and said hello.

"What has you so smiley this morning?" I put the car in reverse and headed into town.

"I was eager to see you, of course, and the baby but I also found this and wanted to pass it along." Megan held up a handmade crocheted elephant.

"Did you make that?" Even though I was focusing on the road I could tell it was well made and gorgeous.

"I did! I used to crochet all the time and then life took over. I don't regret it but I did wonder if I lost the touch. I made one for each of my kids and they cherished it for years. With a bit more time on my hand, I wanted to get back at it and thought your friend's baby was a good reason."

"I'll take one, too."

She missed the meaning and said she could try her hand at nearly anything if I can find the pattern. And then she went silent.

"Wait, does that mean…"

"It does. I wanted to wait to tell you over breakfast, the timing seemed right now though. Where are we going, anyway?"

She squealed in response and then said she didn't care. I could tell that she was shaking with excitement and loved that about her. She was genuine, authentic, and wore her heart on her sleeve and would tell me the truth, always.

I pulled up and parked just outside an all-day breakfast joint. I was in the mood for grease and lots of it. She left the elephant in the car and we went inside.

Once we ordered, she exclaimed, "That's why Travis didn't want you lifting anything today! How are you feeling, are you suffering with morning sickness yet? How far along?"

"Slow down, I'll answer everything." Saying that made my stomach drop as I still didn't decide on what to tell Lucy. "Actually, I'm glad you know now as I have questions for you, too." After our meals arrived and between mouthfuls, I told her everything, including the spotting. "So, I'm just not sure how much to tell Lucy's listeners and my fans yet. With everything so risky, I'm not sure how I would tell the world I lost the baby if that happened."

"Don't talk like that. You'll have this baby. You'll love this baby. He or she is healthy and you're surrounded by people who will make sure you stay that way. I say, tell everything. Be positive and rejoice in the excitement that will follow."

Feeling so much better about having Megan know and be so optimistic, I finished my breakfast without even thinking about being sick and made my decision on what to share on the podcast. I just hoped Travis would be on board.

Chapter Thirty

Megan and I finished eating, she paid the cheque without causing a scene, calling it my "celebratory breakfast". I was very thankful as I still didn't get the chance to check my bank account, and at the thought of that, I realized I abandoned my email for almost twenty-four hours, too.

Once we got to the storage locker Megan told me to sit, that she would load the car by herself and I was just to relax. It felt different, with her doing all of the work, but I took advantage of that time to check my account and emails. Bank first.

I was delighted to see a payment was deposited from advertisements I enabled on my website and it was almost four digits! I let out a squeal of delight and was thankful Megan was at the car so didn't hear. I wasn't sure I wanted to discuss finances and my current stage of penny pinching with her just yet. It was a relief to know I could buy a few things at the used store if I found something special, which I almost always did. I wanted to browse, but planned not to buy, feeling the embarrassment of a declined card at a used clothing store would be too much.

When Megan returned it was just for a moment to grab another box. The box. "Oh, sorry, that one stays." I noticed it was open and crossed my fingers she didn't look inside. And then she did.

"Oh! I can see why."

I peered over, fingers still crossed, and saw that thankfully the doll was missing, but some bottles and toys were making an appearance. I closed it and sat on its edge, sinking a little into the blankets. "It's not what you think. He's going to throw those out and keep the blankets."

"None of my business but that purple one, I recommend holding onto that one," she said with a wink and a giggle then left with another box so I didn't have to react, thank goodness.

I returned my sight to my phone and checked email. Four thousand twenty six unread emails. Deciding they were mostly spam I scrolled to the least recent of the emails and read. It wasn't spam, very few were. The majority were comments on my most recent blog post. Some were offers to sponsor the blog. I picked one of the sponsorship ones and read, not believing it was legitimate. Megan returned and I had her read it. Between us both we read it over seven times and then decided it must be true and I drafted a reply to it.

Lululemon wanted to outfit me in their newest maternity clothes and review it. Plus they offered to pay me, or rather set up an investment fund for my baby. That way they could still legitimately say they were not paying me for glowing reviews but for honest ones. I would be expected to do a post a month dedicated to at least one new outfit, if I found them to be the right fit and I could keep them, of course.

I was all in at first, eager to be outfitted in brand new clothes as I was worried about the price of maternity wear. Before sending the reply I decided to wait, read it over at home and think about it. I didn't want to seem too eager though I did already ignore it for more than a day.

"This is the last box. Want to lock up?"

"Already? Great work. I'll be right behind you." I got up, took a moment to see the now quite empty locker save for the single box, closed and locked the door and met her in the very fully packed car.

"It was like playing Tetris but I got it all to fit."

"That's great! Thank you so much. I should have paid for breakfast, you're the one doing all of the work."

"That's what friends do. Maybe you can find me something at Value Village, though?"

"Sounds like a plan." A manageable one, too, now that I knew I had money.

We had the employee come to the door with a bin and move all of the stuff from the car into the store. We simply stayed put. The staff member came to the passenger side window and knocked. When she rolled it down we were handed a coupon for 20% off future purchases as a show of gratitude. I drove around, found a spot marked for expectant mothers and exclaimed about the luck and wonderful day we were having. It was only 11:12 AM so we still had some time to browse and grab a quick bite before visiting Kate.

We took our time, scrolling through the spines of books and picking out the always recommended "What to Expect When You're Expecting" book as well as a few light reads. Toys next, I found a couple of baby friendly items that seemed appropriate for Candy. Megan suggested not to buy used stuffed animals for fear of mildew and other allergens. I was glad she came with me as I never would have thought of that.

In baby clothes, I found a few adorable newborn sets that looked brand new. The cart was getting pretty full, but we had more exploring to do. We made our way to the board games where I stopped suddenly. Almost convinced my eyes were deceiving me for the at least second time that day. I jumped when Megan ran into me.

"Sorry, what's wrong? I didn't realize you stopped. I was trying to find some games for the boys."

"Don't get this one," I advised as I reached out my finger to a bright pink box. Megan got in close to read it, tilting her head and said aloud, "Naughty Game."

I giggled and excused myself as a senior gentleman walked by. I hoped he was deaf though by the colour of his face realized he heard her loud and clear.

Megan took it from the shelf and started reading the back then began to open it. "Megan, what are you doing? That's not a kid game at all!"

"No, but Chad and I might like it. Or you and Travis."

She was showing me a whole new side of her and I had to admit I kind of liked it. She flipped through the cards, saying she wanted to be sure all the pieces were there, when she dropped the box and everything went flying. "Megan!"

I slowly and carefully bent down to try to fill the box up when a young man, likely a teenager, came to help. I tried to hurry and get the more provocative pieces though, by the sounds of the giggles and gasps, realized I over looked some real good ones. The boy looked mortified as he held up a card to his face. He cleared his throat and apologized, saying that game shouldn't have made it to the shelf. "We usually throw these things out."

Megan gave me a look that clearly said she didn't believe him. We guessed an employee would keep them before throwing them out. "We'll take it!" Megan scrambled to put everything in the box that we could find and refused to let the boy remove it from our cart.

I put a few things on top of it and we hurried away, finding a few more things and went to the cash.

Chapter Thirty-One

In the car, Megan dug through our bags to find the game, determined to find the card the young man was giggling about. It didn't take her long. It was one of the blank cards, where the owner could draw their own activity and the previous owner forgot to erase this one.

We both giggled until we cried, our bellies sore and our hearts full. I would never admit that the image made me a little wet and eager to try. It also made me wish Travis kept his doll. When Megan moved to erase it I grabbed her arm, told her to put it away and I'd go buy lunch before going to the hospital. I was already convinced the game was mine. "Let's have joint custody," she offered. "Every other month this baby is mine with the promise I will always erase our cards."

"First month is mine," I agreed.

We grabbed two kid's meals at a drive-thru, with an added coffee for Kate, neither of us really hungry yet, and made our way to the hospital. In the parking lot, Megan made sure to hide the game from view and to gather a bag full of stuff for Kate, topping it off with her elephant.

Once we arrived on the proper floor, we stopped to ask the nurse which room she was in only, oddly enough, I was reminded again that I didn't know if her last name was the same as Travis' or not. With them moving around so much and living with so many foster families, we weren't confident. Thankfully, Travis came up behind us and we didn't have to answer. He offered to lead the way and carry some of our load.

Entering the room quietly promptly at two, we were surprised to see two other visitors at her bedside. The other beds in the ward of four looked used but were unoccupied. Travis set some things down, peering at the visitors as if trying to place them when Kate explained, "Hey guys, welcome. These are my hospital roommates family, but in my neighbours absence, were just being kind and saying hi." Understanding filled the room as we all exchanged names, congratulations and random polite chatter. Then it got awkward. I recognized them, but hoped they didn't know who I was.

"Anne?"

"Annabelle, now but yes, I thought I recognized you." Turning to the others I explained, "My former landlords. They owned the building I was renting."

"Is this your sister?"

"Umm… no, my friend. Travis is my boyfriend." Mr Stark hid his surprise much better than Mrs Stark, but I could tell they were both immediately judging. Their faces showed strain and surprise and they quickly excused themselves, going to sit in a corner near the opposite bed. I paid them no attention and urged Megan to share her handmade gift with Kate.

"Oh it's gorgeous! Did you make it?"

"I did. I was telling Annabelle that I made one for each of my kids while I was pregnant with them. They still cherish theirs. Each had a slightly different thing about it. It's been a while, so there are a few flaws in yours, I apologize."

"Oh, don't. You'd never be able to tell. It looks perfect and I just love the ribbon sewn in. You'll need to come to the shower. With the move and everything, I delayed it and figured this would make it easier for everyone to meet my princess at the same time. Please, don't bring anything else, though."

"You better not tell me that," I declared. "I'm going to spoil this one as much as I can." Thankful to remember the new flowing income into my account. "We picked up a few things at Value Village while there. I will need to wash them, of course, but I thought I'd show them to you."

After many "aww's" and "what is that?" everything was displayed and packed away again. Mr Stark suddenly appeared behind me and stood in silence. I turned and asked if there was anything I could help him with.

"Yes, in fact. We cleaned out your apartment the other day as we rented it out and found an item." He refused to maintain eye contact no matter how hard I tried. "It was in the back of a drawer, still in a box. Frankly, I don't know how you missed it. We were wondering, well, Mrs Stark was wondering, if you needed it back."

I honestly had no idea what he was referring to, until I did. I felt the colour drain from my face and it suddenly made sense why he was looking at the floor instead of me. "The dildo?" I exclaimed. "Just throw it out or, you can keep it if you want. I think it was a pricey one. I never used it, the seal should still be on the box."

All eyes were on me instead of Kate or the new mother being wheeled into the room. Even the orderlies seemed to slow and stare. "Very well," was all Mr Stark said after a beat and he turned to see his daughter and grandson enter. Not much else was said or done before a nurse came into the room and declared visiting hours over for the afternoon. We each said our goodbyes and, as we exited through the door, Mrs Stark pulled me aside discreetly and whispered, "Thank you. The box was sealed and it's magical," before returning to her husband's side.

I couldn't suppress a giggle, loud enough to have Megan give me a look to which I answered, "I'll explain later." Travis joined us and asked what all the giggling was about. Thankfully Megan jumped in and said that she was just so excited for Kate and for Travis. That she was thankful they all connected and would babysit anytime she could. She also offered her eldest son up for his services, once Candy was a little older. Travis said he'd pass that along and that he knew she'd be grateful. "I do come first, however. Unless I get that job."

"Oh, right! How was the interview?" In all of the excitement I forgot all about it. "Should we got out for a celebratory dinner? Actually, we are going out. Megan, can you join us?"

"I should get home, actually. I'm afraid I'll need to leave you to each other's company." We reached the elevator and she handed Travis the rest of the bags. "Oh, but there's the rest of the stuff in my car. Where are you parked, Travis?"

Looking at his parking stub he declared, "A3, you?"

"B4. Can you drive over to my spot and I can move everything?"

That settled, once we reached the parking garage I went with Megan and Travis when to A3. Once he was out of earshot I told her about the dildo and we were still laughing when he drove up. This time it wasn't so easy to blame it on the excitement of a baby so I showed him the game.

It made him release a giggle and an oo la la, too.

Chapter Thirty-Two

Once we were alone, I asked Travis where he wanted to go and how the interview went. He replied by clicking the option to read the latest text message through the car which said that they would like to make him an offer. I squealed in delight, so happy with such a great day and promising future. "Did you call back?"

"This is actually the first time I'm seeing it. I had my phone on silent at the hospital in case someone was sleeping. Let me call them and see what they will offer."

He called through the phone and was delighted by the offer, I could tell, but he told the man that he'd have to think about it. I had full confidence he was going to take it. I was also very glad he didn't just jump on the first offer as they raised his salary by $2000. He ended the call with a promise to give them an answer in the morning. Once he was sure he hung up and we parked, he leaned over to kiss me. It was awkward and strained, but still magical. We both had a lot to be thankful for.

"Sorry, to answer your first questions, let's eat at Chan's House, I'm starving and in the mood for an all you can eat night. Is that ok?"

"Sounds perfect! I am starving, too." As he drove to the restaurant we couldn't stop holding each other's hands and smiling. It really seemed like the universe had our backs.

"And apparently the interview went well," he answered as he opened my door and gave me a helping hand to the sidewalk. "I'm actually pretty excited. I'm not going to give up on my other applications but this will help."

"I have some news, too," I said quietly. I didn't want to take away from his progress and celebration, but didn't want to hold it back, either. "I got my first deposit from advertisements on my blog." I tried not to give everything away with my face or tone.

Travis paid for parking and then took me by my hand and spun me around, finishing with a dip. The quick action made me a little dizzy, but I enjoyed it and tried not to let Travis see. Once we were seated, I escaped to the washroom just to have a moment to myself. Thankfully it was empty and I sat down on the toilet, after putting the lid down, and took a few deep breaths before hearing the door open. Out of instinct I flushed and opened the stall door, surprised to see Travis standing before me. "You OK?"

"Better now, thanks." Then he kissed me, pushing me against the door I just closed behind me and he reached into my pants. I quickly rewarded his actions with wetness and he entered. I pulled him back into the stall, locked the door and pushed him onto the toilet seat. I awkwardly unzipped his pants as he pulled mine down and, with his fingers pushed my panties aside and I sat down. Dizzy with orgasm, we quietly finished up, oblivious to someone coming into the bathroom. Once we heard a grunt, not of pleasure, we realized how awkward this was.

I left the stall first, a bit disheveled but fully dressed. The plan was for Travis to wait a beat, hopefully giving the third party time to finish and exit before someone else came in. I went back to our table after washing my hands and saw a glass of lemonade was delivered in our absence. Travis had a Coke. I looked around, feeling guilty, but realizing everyone else was just focused on their food, I left the table and filled my plate. Travis still wasn't back so I got back up and filled his with things I thought he'd like.

Returning to the table the second time, I peeked over to the washroom to see a lady coming out. I was anticipating his joining me soon so waited to eat and sipped on my lemonade reliving the event. After waiting twenty minutes, the food long cold and a refill of my lemonade on its way, I returned to the washroom to find Travis fast asleep on the toilet, the stall door not locked.

"Travis!" I whispered loudly as I kicked his foot. "Wake up!"

He woke with a start and then a giggle. He slowly got up and washed his hands, suggesting I leave and lightly knock on the door if the coast was clear. Thankfully, it was and we quickly reunited at the table, our plates absent but my lemonade refilled. We went together to replace our meals with warmer items without a word. Our smirks and winks spoke volumes.

Walking back to the table we sensed correctly that many eyes were on us. Our secret was out somehow and it took me only a few minutes, once I was seated, to discover how. Travis, still standing, forgot to zip up and he was very clearly still excited. His underwear was bulging through the opening. I was mortified but somehow brought his attention to it as discreetly as I could. Once seated, he adjusted and the eyes turned away, but the giggles started.

In an unspoken agreement, we quickly ate our platefuls, left cash on the table and escaped the restaurant. Travis didn't make a sound until we were blocks away when he burst out in laughter.

"Well, that was quite the celebration! It's been a long time since I ate in such silence and so quickly. I'm still hungry, too. You?"

"Starving! Let's get some burgers and eat at home."

"Deal. And thank you for understanding and being so delightful."

We talked then. A lot about Travis's early morning plans to accept the job offer for an interim solution and some about my decision about the podcast and the months ahead. Feeling confident again about our futures, we ate our fast food at the apartment and went to bed.

Chapter Thirty-Three

Life was hectic over the next several months. Travis took the job at the school while still hopeful he'd be in the field in no time.

I did the pod cast, reaping many rewards including enough hype to convince me blogging could be a long term thing. With sponsorships coming in all the time, always looking for honest reviews, new readers subscribing to my YouTube channel and blog daily, and money from advertisements coming in faster than I thought possible, we were settled into a good routine.

Travis hosted a birthday party for me, first offering to take me to the bar as he respected that it was my tradition since I turned of age. I declined. Not being able to drink was only part of that decision. It was time for new traditions, happier ones. We had it at the apartment and it was delightful. Small, intimate and just what I needed.

All the while, baby was growing and I was dealing with all that comes with a first pregnancy. It helped to be distracted by Candy, regularly babysitting her to help Kate maintain her job which was demanding more from her more quickly than expected. She seemed to be a natural in her position and climbed through the ranks as fast as she desired. She didn't want anything too taxing as she wanted as much time with her princess as possible. It was fantastic to see her balance being a single mom and passionate career woman. I aspired to do the same, just much later in life than her.

Travis and I were in a good place, even deciding to rent to own a small house together just outside of the city. It was his birthday present to me. We didn't want to fully commit to buying, still hopeful Travis would land a permanent position and not knowing where it would take us, but we wanted to celebrate our success.

Seven months into my pregnancy I got a scare, though. The worst stomach cramping I had ever experienced and, with everything considered, I was quickly convinced our baby was making an early arrival. I woke up in the middle of a Thursday night, clenching my jaw so tight and reaching for Travis's hand. While I hated waking him up on a school night, this wasn't something I wanted to face alone.

He woke quickly, grabbed my hospital bag and helped me to the car. We didn't even bother changing. He called work on the way, through the car, and left a message saying he wouldn't be in, apologizing for the short notice. Then sent a text to their doctor, as arranged previously. They were not taking any chances.

An auto response came back in seconds from the doctor's office, saying he was out of the office for the week and to contact another doctor. We didn't pay much attention, just made our way to the hospital trusting they would find someone to help.

The pains didn't get worse but they certainly weren't better by the time we arrived. Travis parked in the emergency lot, ran to get me a wheelchair and alert the staff. Accompanied by a security guard who helped lift me into the wheelchair, we felt more at ease already. A nurse met us at the door and told us to follow him. Through clenched eyes and jaw, the nurse seemed vaguely familiar, but I was also a bit delusional from the pain and said nothing. I did grunt though, while at the same time telling the little one it was much too early.

Once I was in the bed, with some help from the nurse and Travis, the nurse introduced himself quickly and said he was going to get the doctor but would be right back. He was back within minutes, asked for my name and exclaimed, "I thought that was you!"

"Excuse me?"

"We went to high school together. Everyone called me Super Jock instead of Jack."

"For good reason," the memories came flooding back. "You were the Jack of All Trades, if I remember correctly, but always an all-around athlete before anything else. I didn't know you stayed local."

"I didn't, actually. I went to LA on a scholarship for basketball. Made it three years, studying sports medicine and then hurt my knee. Too bitter to continue seeing athletes who made it, I switched to gynaecology. Once my mother fell ill, I returned to help take care of her and just stayed. I'm nursing while still training to be a doctor." It was wonderful to hear from a classmate who, too, pivoted later in life, even if he was a success before the big change.

The conversation helped distract me from my pain and I barely noticed the cramps subsiding until Travis mentioned it. "Sorry to interrupt this reunion, but you seem to be feeling better." While they talked, Nurse Jack was setting up monitors which were now reporting the ease of tension.

"They do indeed, Sir. You must be Annabelle's son."

I groaned out of embarrassment for Travis. I hoped this wouldn't continue. "Actually, Travis is the father and this is my first child."

"I'm so sorry. That's one thing I need to learn, bedside manner and not sticking my foot in my mouth. I'll be right back."

"Sorry about that, Travis. That was rude of him."

"No matter, it happens. We'll figure it out. I'm just glad you're feeling better."

The doctor came in then, we didn't see Jack again though I'm not sure if that was intentional on his part or just regular protocol. I was relieved either way. It seemed Travis was, too.

The doctor, a new one, checked me all over and decided it was just Braxton Hicks, that baby and momma were fine and sent us home.

Without the use of a wheelchair this time, yet still feeling week, I sat on a nearby chair while Travis pressed the button for the elevator. While we waited

Jack made another appearance, handing me a piece of paper and telling me he was in charge of our 25 year school reunion and hoped I would attend.

I didn't commit either way before the elevator doors opened and we said our pleasantries and left the hospital.

Chapter Thirty-Four

Now on bed rest for at least a week, doctor's and Travis's orders, I was easily able to catch up on emails and blog posts as well as the book I was reading. With Travis gone the entire day and Megan taking over my babysitting duties, the walls of the big bedroom were closing in fast. Thankful to no longer be in Travis's apartment, we still hadn't made the house our home so the flowered wallpaper was getting on my nerves.

There was only so much Netflix you could binge, so by day three I was ready for some activity. Despite Travis's efforts, laundry was piling up and, if I was careful, I felt fully capable of doing a load or two. Checking the pockets of every piece of clothing out of habit, I was surprised to feel something in my pajama's front pocket. Working my way in I discovered the card Nurse Jack gave me with his number. Forgetting about the laundry, I stared at it as I made my way to sit on the edge of the bed.

Jack was always a good guy. He was popular, gorgeous, very smart and could have any girl he wanted in high school, but he remained kind. My partner in some shared classes, Jack set himself apart from the stereotype and stayed humble. He never once made me feel insecure or dumb, always just his equal despite my clumsiness, awkwardness and general invisibility. And he always remembered my name.

There was one time I was walking down the school hall on my way to class and I dropped my pencil case. Usually I would ensure I squatted instead of bending, always vigilant of who may be looking on but this time I was in a hurry, the halls were fairly empty and I just absent mindedly bent over. It took me a second to grasp my pencil case while balancing my books and in that time I heard a burst of laughter behind me. "She does bend!"

I turned to see a small group of basketball players pointing at me and laughing. The only one who wasn't laughing or pointing was Jack. He didn't even hesitate to break free of the crowd, offering to help me with my books and walk with me to my class despite it making him late for his own and going against the popular crowd. He talked like nothing happened, told me he was proud of me for the work I did on a recent project and, once we got to my classroom, quietly complimented me on my Levi's. I was speechless.

Where moments before I was mortified at the idea of star athletes checking out my ass, I finally had something to be proud of. It seemed genuine, despite my misgivings, he always seemed so authentic so I took it as a compliment and didn't squat again. Instead I proudly bent and did some squats at home to fine tune my behind.

That was the last time those same jock's ever said a mean thing to me, either. They were almost nice after that, if we ever were in the same general area. That moment, however small to Jack, boosted my level of confidence and helped make my high school years more tolerable. I never did thank him for that. It was long overdue, so I as touched the paper with his number I decided I'd give him a call.

Voicemail.

I left my name and number and said it was no hurry, he could call anytime. I wasn't going anywhere and it wasn't a medical call.

Putting the paper on the nightstand to my side of the bed, I returned to the chore at hand and rummaged through more pockets. Besides lint and a few pieces of change, Travis's pockets were empty. It seemed he made sure to clean them every night which, to me, was just a good habit to have and there was nothing suspicious to be thought. So then why did I get a sudden sense of dread?

I started the laundry and moved to the couch for a change of scenery and position. Turning the television on I was surprised to see a still frame of a man entering a woman's behind. Travis and I were open and honest with each other, but also made an agreement to only watch porn together so I was upset. Being seven months pregnant and high risk, I knew I wasn't paying him all the attention he was used to, though I just wanted him to be honest with me about it.

I started up Netflix vowing to myself to talk to him about it later. I found a show and then heard the phone ring. Unfortunately, I left it in the bedroom and by the time I waddled in the rings stopped and a notification popped up about a voicemail. I noticed the number. The call was from Jack but I had yet to figure out how to check for messages so I just called him back.

"Jack? Sorry, I just didn't get to the phone in time. Thanks for calling back."

"Annabelle! I'm so glad you called. I was hoping you would. I'm just on break at school so only have a few minutes. I really want you to help me with this reunion planning."

"I don't know about that. I never went to any of the others. I didn't even go to prom. I won't keep you but I wanted to thank you for something long overdue."

"Thank me?"

"I'm not sure if you remember, but there was a time you really helped me. Your teammates were laughing at me and you stood up, took charge and even paid me a compliment. I don't know if it was even true, but it meant so much to me."

"Nice Levi's," he replied quietly.

"Yes! How do you remember? I totally forgot about it until today."

"It changed my trajectory, too, to be honest. It was the first time I really saw you loosen up. I talked to those boys after, too. I was so mad that they disrespected you that way."

"So it was you. I had to wonder as they were respectful towards me from then on. I wasn't sure if you said something or they just smartened up on their own."

"We'll talk about it more soon, but I have to go for now. Call me again, Annabelle. Until then, I'll be waiting to hear your voice again. It's been too many years."

He hung up as I remained frozen in place, bringing the phone slowly to eye sight and just stared. How did I change his trajectory of life? I don't even remember saying anything as we walked.

I finally pressed the end button when the annoying beeping got to be too much. Still staring at the phone I realized the time and that Travis would be home soon. I switched the laundry and then put together a charcuterie plate for his arrival. It was an odd one, nothing to take a picture of for InstaGram, but I had to make do with what we had.

After I set it on the coffee table, I started making a grocery list and then he came home.

Chapter Thirty-Five

"What are you doing up? You're supposed to be on bed rest?"

"I was so bored and sore from just lying there. I had to get up. I was careful, I promise." I welcomed him with our ritualistic kiss on the cheek, me no longer feeling like participating in foreplay every time we saw each other. I hoped it was just a phase that would pass once the little one was born, or soon after, and I knew Travis did, too.

I wasn't sure how to best approach my finding porn on the living room television so I braced for a fight when I just came out with it. As I set the food before him on the coffee table, I asked why he was watching porn without me. It was clear I caught him off guard as he struggled to get words out. Typically my first question was 'how was your day' but I didn't care at that point.

"Baby, I'm sorry. I've been so lonely and needed a release. I figured it was better than bothering you. I've been so stressed lately."

"You've been stressed?" I couldn't believe it. This was the first time he even mentioned even being worried. I was pissed while also feeling guilty for being so mad. "What about me? I'm not even allowed to leave the apartment or shop for baby clothes. I can't even drive!" It was odd for me to say that when so recently I was terrified to get behind the wheel. "And this little one will be here in less than two months. I barely see anyone, I'm always sore and yes, I would love a little action, too, once in a while. Instead I feel like a caged animal blessed with visitors on occasion. But you're stressed and need to relax."

"You're absolutely right. I know that and that's why I didn't say anything. But with teaching, preparing, taking care of you…"

"Oh Travis. Sorry to be such a burden to you." This was our first fight, and it was just getting started. "Excuse me while I make it easier for you and move into the other room. I'll clean up my mess once the baby arrives."

With that I grabbed a plate of food and escaped to the other room. Unfortunately that room didn't have a television but it did have books. And it didn't have Travis until he stormed in yelling about a voicemail.

"Who is Jack? And don't you know how to check our damn voicemail yet? On top of everything else, you expect me to come home and check messages from your other men."

I froze. I never saw this side of Travis. Even when I was seeing other men at the same time as him. When that was happening, it just seemed to strengthen his resolve to woo me better. His jealousy fueled him, but now it was another beast entirely.

"Travis, take a breath. It's innocent. You met Jack. He was the nurse at the hospital last week.

Remember the guy I went to high school with?" I hoped I could calm him quickly as I'm sure the yelling and my increasing blood pressure wasn't good for our baby.

"Why is he calling? Is everything alright with the baby?" Once he thought it might be medical he calmed down a notch, his voice dropped in volume and I was able to breathe.

"He was returning my call, actually. Travis, he was a friend, but that's all. I'm allowed to have friends, right? It really was nothing."

"So why didn't you tell me? You said nothing about wanting to call him. You didn't even mention him this week. How many times have you talked to him?"

"Not that it's any of your business, but I did a load of laundry and found his number in my pocket…"

"You did laundry? You are supposed to be on bedrest. What don't you get about that?"

"And what don't you get about taking a breath and speaking to me nicely. You know the baby can hear you, right? And feel the tension?"

"Don't you lecture me! We're reading all of the same books. I know everything that you do."

"Then calm down, please." I patted the bed beside me, inviting him to sit down. "Travis, what's going on? This can't be all about Jack?"

That was all he needed to unload on me. Explaining that he was worried about me, the baby, becoming a father. He was frustrated that he wasn't getting any call backs from the jobs in the field he was applying for. Some of his students were giving him a hard time and he hated being away from me and his niece. He had planned to do so much more, but also so much less. Though rare, he once again brought up his age and how most people his age were living life. He was still putting in some shifts at the bar when Jack couldn't find someone and everyone he tended to was his age. Having the time of their life while he was settling down, thinking about buying a house and wondering if he should be purposing and planning a wedding.

"I can answer only one of those things. I don't want to get married. Not now. Maybe not ever."

A tear fell from Travis then. I never saw him cry before, though he was close when he witnessed his niece being born. It was sweet but also troubling. "So you don't want to marry me?"

Good gracious, this wasn't the time to have this conversation. He was so tired, I was exhausted and this was the first time marriage was even mentioned. We just had so many other things to talk about.

"Travis, I love you. I want to be with you. Forever or longer. I'm just not a huge supporter of marriage. Who would we even invite? Since my parents died, I just didn't see the point in adding such an expense to my life for a piece of paper and a party with so few people. It's not you, it's me."

His tears stopped and he leaned over to kiss me then, bad breath and all. I kissed back and we somehow awkwardly made up by making out. He was the most tender I had ever seen him and I quickly found myself stripping him, then me, and making love to him so very carefully. My protruding belly and extra 20 lbs of fat be damned.

Without getting dressed we fell asleep in each other's arms, spent from the fight and odd love making. The fight and discussion weren't over, just over for now.

Chapter Thirty-Six

Travis got up early and snuck out of bed in attempt to leave me sleeping but I was wide awake. I pretended to be sleeping as, through my mostly sleepless night, I came up with a plan and needed Travis's cell phone to help. Though his usual routine was to take his phone to the bathroom, he didn't charge it through the night so I assumed he would leave it on our bedroom charger while he showered. Once I heard the bathroom door close I snuck into our room, with the excuse of being more comfortable in our bed at the tip of my tongue.

Fortunately I was right and his phone was on the charger on his nightstand. I crawled under the covers and leaned over to his side, grabbing his phone but keeping it connected to the charger. I scrolled through his contacts and found the one I wanted. I took a picture of it using my phone and put the phones back just in time for Travis to get out of the shower. Unfortunately, I forgot to turn off his screen and he noticed right away.

"Were you on my phone?"

Dammit!

Not being able to think quickly so early I mumbled something about thinking it was mine. "I turned it on and immediately realized it was yours. Sorry."

I couldn't tell if he was satisfied with that lame excuse or not as I kept my eyes away and made like I was going back to sleep. Which was actually the plan but I had a call to make first.

Travis tucked me in, kissed me on the forehead and warned me to take it easy. He got me new books from the shelf, leaving them on the nightstand as a way of gently telling me not to leave the bed. It was equally sweet and annoying as I was no kept woman. I knew how to take care of myself, sort of.

Once he left I called Jack from my cell phone. I felt guilty, as if I was doing something I shouldn't be, though I knew I wasn't. It was innocent. I just wanted to chat with him about the reunion without sparking another Travis meltdown. I would tell him about it, of course but by the time I did, he would love the idea I had and my status would be increased again, I hoped.

"Jack, I'm glad I caught you. I wanted to ask when you would be available to meet me for dinner to talk about the reunion."

"Annabelle! I was just thinking about you. How about Sunday?"

Thinking about my release date from bed confinement, I realized that would work perfectly and agreed. We would meet at Rocco's Sunday night. With that decided, my real work would begin, just after another nap.

I couldn't get back to sleep like I had planned so gave up trying. I made some toast, grabbed a banana and orange juice and returned to bed. Once my toast was eaten I called Travis's friend, using the number from the picture I took.

"Mitchell? It's Annabelle, Travis's girlfriend." Even after all those months later it seemed like such an odd term. "We met at his birthday party." I waited a second for his memory to place me.

"Oh, hey. How are you?"

"I hope I didn't catch you at a bad time. I wanted to see if you would be interested in hosting a diaper party for Travis Sunday evening. Nothing complicated. It's much like a baby shower but the men bring diapers of all sizes and have some drinks together. He needs a night out and where there is no classes Monday, it should work well."

"This would be my first but yeah, I can get some of the guys together and figure out what diapers to bring. Thanks for reaching out. I'll message him with a time and place later today."

"Perfect. Thanks so much. Please don't tell him it was my idea. I want it to be a surprise. You can take all the credit!" He agreed with a chuckle confirming that he would, assuring that he would take the blame if it turned out terribly, too."

Everything was working smoothly, it seemed. I knew Kate was planning a shower for me soon though all the details were kept secret. It was fun to be the centre of attention for once, to be the one kept out of the loop to be surprised. And to have friends to put in that effort.

While I was still exhausted, the excitement of having plans in motion kept me buzzing so I tidied up the place, wrote a blog and caught up on some emails. I was delighted each day to see my audience growing and my request for sponsorships expanding. Everything from food to make up to clothing and offers to speak at events; what started as a little creative project was turning into a successful career where I had the flexibility to say no and choose my hours and location.

Yes, of course, there were some sketchy emails and comments, some inappropriate requests that I needed to block, but overall it was the best decision I ever made. Tara even offered to do a pregnancy photo shoot, with Travis, which was out of her normal clientele. She was so flattered with my review she wanted to shoot us again for free. I had already found some lingerie to wear, we just needed to schedule a time and it had to be soon.

It was getting harder to ensure everything was done before our baby's arrival, especially with me on bedrest but we had our crib, Travis just needed to assemble it, and a car seat as well as stroller plus a few clothing items. Some things in duplicate because they were given to me for review which was wonderful. It meant that although we didn't get to choose our preferred items, we were saving a lot of money and had some options. Not to mention, we were saving a bundle while still getting top of the line items. Except for that one stroller which was recalled due to wheels falling off which I mentioned In my review they still insisted I write honestly. I guess they still thought even bad publicity was good publicity. We threw it out, thankful we had two reliable ones on standby.

It felt good to be able to provide and not be stuck at the office for forty hours a week though not having benefits, especially these days, was troublesome. Thankfully, Travis's insurance covered a lot of what we needed so far.

I was on the phone most of the day, scheduling a hair appointment, booking the photo shoot with Tara for the next day, and a car appointment to ensure it was fully inspected. I also made a list of meals we could make and freeze in advance to ensure it was easier to eat easily and healthy after the arrival.

Travis arrived home and was, once again, furious. I paid him minimal attention, telling him our appointment with Tara was at 2 PM the next day and just went to bed. The day exhausted me and I wasn't in the mood for his despair.

Chapter Thirty-Seven

I sensed, more than saw, the shift in Travis's mood when he came to bed. I was just barely asleep when he came in whistling. It wasn't the whistle that bothered me as much as the crinkling of the bag of chips he was carrying. Not only did I hate that he ate in bed, typically while watching a movie, but the noise of him eating was too much.

I wished I talked to him about it. Wished I mentioned that he should go to the couch and respect that I was sleeping, but I got up instead and made my way to the other room without a word. I grabbed a drink on the way and when I turned he was standing there, silent, staring at me. "Something wrong?"

His voice was huskier than usual which made me wonder if he was drinking. Months earlier he agreed to cut back considerably in solidarity with my restrictions, but it wasn't that. There was something off about him I couldn't quite place. "I was just tired and you woke me up coming in."

"Something wrong?" he repeated without moving or even blinking.

He was sleep walking, and talking, apparently. He warned me of the possibility, but I never saw it firsthand. From what I knew, it was best to let the situation play out. I didn't want to pry, poke or disturb him, but I was curious. "Not with me. You?"

"I don't want you seeing him."

I thought I knew who he was referring to though asked anyway, "Who?"

"Super Jock. He isn't good for you. I'm good for you." With that he slammed his hand on the counter and literally woke himself up. He looked surprised and confused while I pretended I wasn't just talking to him. "Ready for bed?" he asked innocently.

"Sure am," I replied, deciding to give him a break and sleep in the same bed. I laid awake long after he was snoring, considering my options. I could ask him about it in the morning, hash it out and move on. On the other hand, it was sleep walking and talking Travis, maybe he meant nothing by it and I should let it slide. I fell asleep with only one decision made – to research sleep walking.

I had a ton of questions to consider and wasn't sure if there was one right one. Like – would he remember this in the morning? Is he really worried about Jack? Is sleep walking hereditary? Did I have something to worry about?

I fell asleep somehow and woke to the sound of him in the shower. Puzzled at first, unaware of the time, I wondered for a second if he was still asleep. I never dealt with this before, anything seemed possible. I waited until he left to start my research. He didn't tell me where he was going and I didn't bother to ask. We tried to spend weekends together, but I also knew he needed time to himself. I just worried he wouldn't be back for our appointment or wouldn't remember so I texted him.

As I waited for his reply, I began my research which resulted in learning a lot of conflicting information and being no further ahead in understanding what happened, what may happen or how best to deal with it. Travis still hadn't returned so I wrote a post then turned on the television, starting to worry about his extended absence and that he wouldn't make it back.

An episode of something played before me while my mind was focused on other things. I started getting clothes ready for my time with Tara, committed to going without Travis. I dreaded it but remembered how comfortable Tara had made me feel last time. Always a worrier, having to deal with everything pregnancy and new relationship related wasn't helpful with my level of worry. I was relieved when the door opened and Travis stood there with bags full of baby items and a bit smile.

"I needed to go shopping. To be alone, really, and I thought a lot about you and our little one. They have the cutest things now. I also bought some things for the photo shoot"

"I'm glad you're home." I was. I was so very relieved and felt my worry melt away.

"I brought lunch, too. I hope burgers are OK."

"Sounds good," I said, realizing I didn't eat all day and baby wanted red meat apparently. He was kicking up a storm which was delightful and annoying. I grabbed Travis's hand and rested on the most kicked area of my belly. He felt the kicks before, was even around for an episode of hiccups – the baby's, not mine – it was just important to both of us he felt the baby as much as possible. He was always so sweet when he did.

"Oh, and I am going out tomorrow night. Jack, my boss from the bar not your Jack, or rather, not Jock, texted me; something about a diaper party. He said he got a few of the guys to come out. I hope that's OK."

Of course it was OK, it was my idea. I thought it odd the invite came from his boss, but assumed Mitchell and him were friends and was happy they were both going. Travis's statement also created another guilt trip as I wasn't sure if I should tell him I was going out, too. And with "my Jack/ Jock". I decided against it for now and hoped he didn't realize it would be my first day of freedom as then he might have cancelled.

Our food arrived and we ate the best meal together in a long time. We were both very full, so thankful we had some time before we had to leave for Tara's.

We took that time to pick out some options for Travis to wear, knowing men were not Tara's usual clientele so she wasn't prepared to dress him. It was peaceful, delightful and healing. I actually found myself getting excited about having my picture taken.

It was time to go.

Chapter Thirty-Eight

Tara was by herself, as it was usually her day off all her staff was home. She welcomed us in with excitement and glee which made me relax even more. She looked through my bag, clothes flying everywhere, until she landed on something that caught her eye. I was thrilled as it was the one I was hoping for. "This inspires me! Go change," she said as she flung it at me.

Not bothering to go behind the curtain, I changed into the lingerie as she turned on and adjusted her lighting, talking the whole time. "Travis. I'll have you stand aside for this one and join her for a few shots once I get some solo ones," she said as she worked.

He stayed quiet, shrunk in the corner and watched as I posed and moved as instructed with a smile on my face almost the entire time. Tara asked me to suppress the smile for some more serious shots and she took some close ups of my exposed belly, even zooming in on my outie belly button. I had no idea what these would turn out to look like, but the experience put me at ease and made me feel like a queen. It was entirely needed.

After a while, before changing wardrobe, Tara invited Travis in. "What do I wear?" he asked meekly.

"Hmm… why don't we get you down to your boxers for some. We'll see how it goes."

He went behind the curtain and took longer than I would have expected but came out timidly and stood behind me. We did some of the corny poses we saw from a lot of pregnancy photo shoots, only with less clothes. We were maneuvered and sat on strange furniture as Tara clicked happily and talked, telling us how much research she did for our shoot and how much she learned. She was even entertaining the idea of offering pregnancy shoots to others if these turned out well.

Hours passed, clothes were changed, and lights were dimmed and brightened. The afternoon passed quickly and I really felt a connection with Tara that went beyond photographer and model. There were a few moments that I needed a break, plenty of bathroom stops, and every time I returned I was happy to see Travis more comfortable and chatty.

I was so embarrassed with my passing gas several times and Tara told me not to worry, farting herself and laughing it off. Travis seemed dumbfounded and tried to ignore our antics.

And then the worst happened and I felt terrible.

The door to the studio swung open abruptly, banging against the wall and the motion blew a bag of feathers all over Travis and me. A dog came tumbling in, smashed into a tub of glitter which covered the feathers and our bodies. Bursting into laughter and with such a weak bladder I couldn't hold it back and urine came rainbowing out all over Travis, the pillows and even on the dog. Tara ran around, trying to get the dog out while apologizing and trying to make light of the entire situation.

I'm not sure who felt worse – Tara for letting the intrusion happen or me, but I would place bets on me. I looked to be even more mortified that the camera kept going, realizing she had one set to continue shooting so she could have some candid shots. Great business idea but she was now just wasting so much of her memory card getting weird shots.

"I guess Willow here thinks I have enough shots and needs attention. I love her confidence and we'll go with that. I'm so sorry she interrupted. I completely spaced on latching the door. I do have over 500 shots, though, we'll find something."

I excused myself to the washroom, cleaning myself up and getting dressed after handing Travis a soapy cloth to wipe his leg. He did and got dressed behind the curtain while Tara scrambled to get the dog out and start cleaning up. Thankfully the smell of urine wasn't strong as I was drinking lots of water and going lots.

Once dressed, I came out with another cloth and spray, apologizing profusely and promising to replace or refund the amount of whatever it cost for what I ruined.

"Don't worry about it. I think you only got one pillow and it was my fault."

"Let me at least treat you to a supper out then, soon. Or maybe not so soon depending on the arrival of my little one," I tried to bend over and clean what I could, but it was obvious I was struggling. Tara took the items from my hand and told me to go home.

Travis came out from behind the curtain, gathered up the clothing that was all over and packed it back in our bag. Helping me into my shoes and then out to the car he barely said anything else, to Tara or me.

Once home we both showered and threw our clothes, all of them, in the laundry bin. He started a load of laundry and cooked some pasta. His silence was still obvious but I was too exhausted to push him.

Afterwards we just chilled and watched Netflix until Kate came over. We loved her weekly visits and it gave her time to herself. Travis was so good to Candy it was wonderful to see. I was jealous I wasn't able to do much with her though it seemed he made up for my absence.

It was a good and full day, filled with laughter and smiles. I felt better than I had in a while and we both slept well. Things seemed good again and for that I was thankful. I was hopeful this would be the turn we needed.

Even though I was up five times throughout the night to rid myself of just one glass of water I drank before 8:00 PM, Travis didn't stir, walk or talk. He was sound asleep. I tried to watch him a little each time I returned to bed though was unsuccessful, falling back to sleep very quickly each time.

For as peaceful and civil as we were that night, I wish I had realized it was the calm before the storm.

Chapter Thirty-Nine

The day passed quickly and the peace continued. There was no mention Jack or my doing too much. Travis even had a bouquet of flowers delivered with dual purpose – one to celebrate my week of no pregnancy scares and doing well on bed rest, second because he was leaving me alone on my first night of freedom.

To alleviate his guilt I did finally admit to being invited out to supper with a friend. Being general seemed the best way to go. I wasn't lying to him that way and I wouldn't have him worked up. I wanted him to be as relaxed as possible and enjoy his night out. It might be the last for us both for some time.

We started getting ready at the same time though I was encouraging him to get out the door first. I was fretting about what to wear; not wanting to be too flirty while also not being the prude Jack may remember from school. My free maternity wear was limited but there were a few pieces I still looked great in. I put on one of the dresses and put off putting make up and doing my hair until after Travis left.

"Wowee," he exclaimed when he came into the room.

"You're looking quite handsome yourself, stud. I hope your friends realize you don't have time for three babies."

He looked puzzled at first. I wasn't great at this flirting thing, even still, and then he got it and laughed. "Just you and our baby, I promise. Well, and then Kate and Candy, we can't forget about those two."

I kissed him, as hard as I could with the belly keeping us separated. We only stopped when we heard a knock at the door. "It must be your Jack. Go, have fun. Stay out as late as you need. I'll be here when you get back."

He kissed me again and walked away holding my hand until the very last second. Like kids we blew kisses to each other as he exited and I checked my watch as soon as the door closed. I had just fifteen minutes before I followed him out. I only needed five for the bit of make-up I planned, but getting my hair looking like I wanted might make me late.

It did, but just fashionably, and I found I was actually impressed with how everything looked. I spotted Jack as soon as I stepped into the restaurant as he was hard to miss. He looked fine! And stood politely beside the table by the window as I approached. He reached over to pull my chair out.

"It was such a nice night, I thought a window seat would be fitting." I looked out at the gorgeous view of the well-lit park and agreed.

"It's beautiful. I don't know if I ever saw the park from this view."

"You're beautiful, too, Annabelle. I can't believe our luck with connecting again. It has seriously been too long."

We chatted, ordered, ate delicious meals and continued to talk over drinks for an hour more. Time was passing as if nothing else in the world mattered and like the over twenty years was only seconds. We caught up on who we stayed in touch with, he told me about his marriage and what went wrong. I told him about turning forty and finally embracing life as I should have been all along.

We talked about our future plans, our dreams and memories of school. Our favourite teachers, who passed and who inspired us the most. It was surprisingly and delightfully familiar and comfortable. I was worried things would be awkward and we would have nothing in common, but it wasn't like that at all. I found a new old friend and loved it.

When it was time to part ways, with the restaurant trying to close, Jack insisted on paying. I only agreed if he let me leave the tip. In the hustle of getting up, his wallet fell off the table. I apologized for not being in a position to pick it up and actually sat down again quickly. A spell of dizziness hit me from getting up so fast. He forgave me, and as he bent down to get his wallet he reached out and checked my pulse through my wrist.

He commented that the beat was fast but not abnormally so and stood. The entire scene was over in less than a minute, and while he paid I made one last pit stop to the washroom. Standing back up slowly I felt much more stable.

In the stall I heard yelling and worried. I debated whether or not I should hurry up or stay silent and hide. I finished up and slowly opened the main bathroom door to peek out and see two men fighting by the cash register. I recognized one as Jack almost immediately, even with his back facing me and then I recognized the voice of the aggressor.

"Travis!" I waddled out as quickly as I could manage. "What are you doing here?"

He calmed down only slightly. "I could ask you the same thing!" His voice was strained, a little more than a whisper, but he seemed to be resisting a yell.

"I told you. I was meeting a friend for dinner. We were just leaving."

"With Super Jock?" His volume was getting higher but he was still trying to hold back. "It's 9:00 PM, you need to be home."

"No, I need to be enjoying my night, as do you. And we do not need to be making such a scene at such a nice establishment. This lady wants to close, is just waiting for us to pay. If you need to say anything more you'll wait outside and down the street. Joey, go cool him down. We will be right out."

I had no idea what sparked this. It seemed to be much more than my not saying which friend I would be dining with. Apologizing to the staff for my boyfriend's intrusion and ignorance, I left them more for a tip.

Before exiting, I turned to Jack and apologized, looking him all over to ensure he wasn't hurt physically.

"This makes no sense. I had never seen this side of him before. I don't get it and there is no excuse. I understand if you want to leave now though I would feel safer if you stayed. I also want to make him apologize to you, for what that might be worth."

"I'm not leaving you with him like that. Let's go see what has him so upset. And figure out why he's not living it up with his boys."

Chapter Forty

As we approached I almost burst out laughing. If the situation wasn't so seriously confusing and tense, I would have laughed until I peed. Which really wouldn't have taken much. Here were four manly men standing at a corner of a practically deserted street with bags and packages of diapers at their feet. Everything just looked so ludicrous, especially their strained faces and hushed banter.

"Where is the ring?" Travis yelled as I approached. "I saw the jerk propose. Who asks a pregnant woman to marry them after not seeing her for twenty years?"

I was confused as hell and baffled when he took both of my hands, looked them over and drop them. "What ring? What are you talking about?" And then it dawned on me. He must have saw us through the window when Jack bent down to get his wallet. From the side view it would very much look like a proposal. "Travis, you have it all wrong. We're just friends."

"No we're not. You're the mother of my first child. You are my everything. You are more than my friend."

"Jack and I. Jack and I are just friends. I'm with you." The situation, of course, was so ridiculous and made more so by the amount of alcohol Travis enjoyed with his friends. One approached, someone I never met before, and apologized on Travis's behalf.

"He's had far too much to drink. He will likely not even remember this by morning. It's my fault. It has been years. Far too long and I knew it would be awhile before he could enjoy himself like this again. I shouldn't have been so irresponsible. Our timing was completely wrong. Let me take him back to my place tonight. I'll let him dry out and get him back to you in the morning. I'm FRIEND, by the way. We grew up together."

The name sounded so familiar and then it hit me. Standing before me was Rubber Doll man. I had to laugh that time, despite it being very inappropriate to do so. After the story Travis told I hoped I wouldn't need to face Rubber Doll Man, ever yet here he was. I was delighted for Travis reconnecting with him, however.

Not seeing anything wrong with his offer and being relieved I wouldn't have to deal with his drunkenness anymore, I agreed. I thanked him and apologized for my outburst, blaming it on the pregnancy hormones.

My Jack walked me to my car and offered to follow me home. I didn't see any harm in it and felt better about having him ensure Travis didn't convince his friends he should just go home so agreed. He followed closely and pulled in right behind me, with traffic limited at that hour it wasn't a challenge.

Once we arrived I got out quickly and waved to him, expecting him to stay in his car and just drive to his place. Instead when I turned, I saw him getting out and walking towards me. "I didn't want to miss another chance to hug you," he said quietly as he approached. "I hope I'm not being too forward."

He was but I didn't mind. I knew Travis would, especially tonight, and while we didn't know our neighbours well yet, I was worried what they would say so invited him in. "Sorry, didn't want the nosy neighbours to see and upset Travis again." I hugged him once the door was closed and it lasted much longer than a normal hug did. Then again, I didn't receive many hugs to be able to know what was considered normal. As awkward as it was with my protruding belly, it was also wonderful and comfortable. Before we released, I noticed our heart beats matched the same rhythm which was slow and strong. It relaxed me.

"Do you want a coffee or any other beverage?" It made me feel so much better with him there. Since committing to Travis, my nights alone were minimal and, since moving into the house, were non-existent.

He seemed hesitant, but then agreed. Despite the caffeine for him and the excitement and stress of the night for me, somehow we both fell asleep on the couch. I woke to the sensation of someone watching me and startled to see that it was true.

Travis was standing over me with his hands on his hips, taking deep breaths in and letting them out slowly. I sat up, awkwardly as I realized my legs were entwined with Jack's. The events of the night before hit me like a brick as I muttered, "Let me explain."

Travis held out his hand to aide me in standing up. Once I was on my feet and somewhat stable, I leaned over to gently poke Jack, trying to wake him from what seemed to be a very deep sleep. Travis decided on a different tactic and yelled for him to get out of his house.

The raised voice and abrupt rudeness startled me as much as it did Jack. I looked at Travis, struck by his continued terrible attitude and was thankful I didn't even switch to pajamas.

"Travis, nothing happened. You're being ridiculous."

Jack defended me before Travis could say anything more. "Annabelle, you do not need to explain. It's clear I'm not welcome here and Travis is being a jerk. Nothing happened, man. I was being a friend to her and you're being an asshole. I'll leave when Annabelle says she's OK with it."

Jack read me seemingly better than Travis was in that moment. He seemed to sense my nervousness of being left alone with Travis as worked up as he was. I never saw him like that before and being alone with him wasn't something I wanted right then.

I didn't realize I wouldn't be alone with him much more at all so should have been careful what I wished for.

As Travis and Jack argued I escaped to the kitchen for a glass of water. I knew Jack could handle himself and didn't need the baby hearing all the drama. Pouring the water into a glass I wiggled, realizing I needed to pee more than drink. And then I felt a tightness in my stomach like never before and my legs warmed with urine.

The glass slipped from my hand and shattered in the sink as I grabbed the edge of the counter and moaned through the pain. It was embarrassing but happening nonetheless and I was very grateful to have Jack there. "Ummm, guys?" I beckoned as the pain subsided. "Can someone help me?"

They both came running in. Travis, a step ahead of Jack, almost slipped on my urine but managed to stay on his feet. "What happened?" He looked around at the mess and came to the same conclusion I did, "Did you not make it to the bathroom? Are you ok?"

Jack came to another conclusion. "That's not urine, Annabelle. Your water broke."

Chapter Forty-One

Travis gasped and I moaned, another contraction hitting fast. "It's too early for this. Do I call an ambulance? Is this another Braxton Hicks episode? I'll get your bag." Travis was talking so fast it was hard to keep up. Jack stayed calm and took my hand, helping me lay on the ceramic tiles not drenched by the liquid.

"Travis, calm down man. We need you to take a breath."

"Me?" I asked naively.

"Well, yes, you and Travis. This baby doesn't seem to care how far along you are or when you think it's time, it's coming now. We may not even have time to go to the hospital."

"We have to, I have her bag packed. They are expecting us. Doctor Gee told us to call anytime and he'd be there. It's too risky to have here."

"Travis!" Jack finally raised his voice but it didn't seem to be from frustration, simply necessity. "I need to focus on Annabelle and your baby, not you. You need to seriously calm down. I've done this before. Things will be ok."

With his words to Travis I felt a fraction of relief. My body was screaming to me that there was no time to go to the hospital, baby was being born at home. Between clenched teeth, immense pain and disbelief, I reached for Travis and looked him in the eye. "Please, I need you to do what Jack says. I love you, despite your flaws, but he is the professional here. Let him help and listen to what he says."

I finished my plea with a scream as my contractions worsened. "Travis, go get her a pillow, some towels and put a pot of water onto boil. Then call an ambulance."

Travis left the room and I heard him slamming doors and drawers between screams and Jack's attempts at calming me. He guided my knees up and legs apart then apologized but said he'd need to take my bottoms off, including underwear. He struggled as he closed his eyes to do it as I tried to help. It wasn't an easy task, nor quick, and Travis was back in the room which made it even worse. "Let me do that," he said calmer than I expected.

"Good gracious, if he's delivering our baby he's going to be seeing all of me. Grow up!" It was the first time I used those words on Travis but he was being a lot more immature than I've seen him, even when he was drinking.

Jack cringed but stayed silent. He was clearly trying to be the better man; professional yet sympathetic to the situation. Travis pushed him out of the way, forcibly took down my pajama pants and panties and then went back to his task of filling a pot with water. Once he had it set, he reported that the ambulance was on his way.

"Did they not ask you to stay on the line?" I noticed he didn't have the phone in his hand.

"Oh shoot, they did. I just set it down and forgot to pick it up," he said as he rushed out of the kitchen in search of the phone.

When Travis returned, the water was boiling and Jack asked him to put a pair of scissors in it. He did despite all the confusion. He seemed calmer with a list of tasks to complete. When he returned to my side I could smell the sweat dripping from his skin. As soon as he kneeled down we all heard a knock at the door. "It must be the ambulance," Travis announced.

"I didn't hear any sirens," Jack said to no one in particular. He turned to me and declared that they were too late, it was time to push, but that they would take me to the hospital once done.

"Annabelle? Did you forget about your appointment this morning?"

Lucy was standing in the doorway to the kitchen, making an effort to look right at my face though was failing miserably.

"Shit! I forgot all about it. Lucy, we'll need to take a rain check."

"Oh, I don't think so. You clearly need someone to hold your other hand." Travis and Lucy took sides and let me squeeze their hands through my pain. Soon after I looked to see two more people had entered the kitchen to make an audience. I was mortified though really didn't have time to get dressed or make tea.

Something was burning. We all smelled it though I was the only one it seemed who was holding back some vomit. It took a minute to realize it was the pot with the scissors, now void of water while still on a burner turned to high. One paramedic stood and turned it off while the other sat down at the table in the dining room, which was simply an extension of the kitchen, and pulled out some knitting. It caught me off guard, seeing a man in uniform knitting while I was in such a way, though I realized nothing about this situation was typical.

As a distraction I watched the man go through the motions of his knitting project and it took me back to watching my mother knit. It was meditative and I always wanted to learn how to, just never got around to it.

"PUSH!" I heard Jack yell, as if from a distance, and my body reacted with an awkward upheaval of what energy I had left. My eyes stayed focused on the melodic motions of knitting needles hitting together. The yarn was a light green. Gender neutral, I thought. Calming.

And then the room was even more chaotic as I heard a baby scream. The audience gathered around me, the knitter put his project back in a bag and took the baby from Jack, but didn't go far. The other paramedic bent beside me with scissors just as Travis got up for the ones he previously boiled to sanitize.

"Chris, let Travis do the honours," Jack urged. "He's the father, after all, and does seem much calmer now."

Chris must be the paramedic I thought before passing out, likely from exertion and lack of nutrients as it felt like I hadn't eaten in days. Or maybe I just blanked out and it wasn't medical. Just exhaustion. I barely saw that Travis was cutting the umbilical cord with scissors from the paramedic's bag. Vaguely watched as Jack held a sack of something in his hand. Once I was loaded onto a bed I was handed our little one, free from me but forever linked.

I held her tight as I was lifted into the ambulance. Watching Travis try to get in after the paramedics. They blocked him. Told him to meet us at the hospital. Clarified that their lights would be on, as well as sirens, but their speed would be at the designated limit unless something went wrong.

"Jack, you coming?"

The colour of Travis's face darkened as the doors closed with Jack inside.

I couldn't stress about it now. I had a beautiful baby to look at. One who looked exactly like Travis in all of the right ways. It was such a relief to see the resemblance and not have to worry about Chuck anymore.

I knew that pretty soon I wouldn't have to worry about Mike either. His court date was nearing.

Chapter Forty-Two

Thankfully, nothing went wrong on the way. The ride seemed to take forever and the sirens deafening but I didn't really care. I had a healthy baby, finally some pain relief and peace of mind. Once we got to the hospital Travis and Jack arrived in my room, along with Lucy, Kate, Candy and Megan all within 15 minutes. Thankfully I was freshened up a little and in a gown by then, but still bed ridden and being poked and prodded by doctors.

One doctor took our little one away for further testing. While the Apgar test was done on the way and everything seemed fine, they could never be too sure. Doctor Gee took the placenta that was contained in a cooler, too and I thought to ask why, but really wasn't sure I wanted to know. If anything was concerning or important, I was confident they would tell me.

The knitting paramedic returned, which I thought unusual until he presented me with the final project. Apparently he took great pride in knitting hats for the babies he takes part in delivering and always knits them in the same light green. It may have been the hormones or the fact that it was such an emotional day. Whatever it was, his tradition sent me into a blubbering mess and my eyes were pools of water. Despite that, I did not miss his look towards Jack and I giggled. It all seemed so perfect. I didn't say a word.

I did, however, feel all tingly when Jack and the paramedic left the room together and again when Jack appeared a few minutes with a smile on his face and a skip in his step.

Travis didn't leave my side and was ever the gentleman once again, which put me at ease. After a lot of conversation and gift giving, I realized I was hungry and asked Travis to get a snack from the packed hospital bag. All of my favourite healthy snacks were included, and approved by the doctor in advance. We made sure to pack all peanut free ones as we knew I'd be eventually sharing a room to save on funds. And we wouldn't want to risk a newborn or new mom having an allergic reaction.

I was surprised to hear Travis say "Oh dear!" when he opened the bag. I couldn't see what he was going, too attached to machines to comfortable twist, but heard him rummaging and then laughing. "I think I must have grabbed the wrong bag," he said as he lifted the game from Value Village in the air. I took a peak in and saw the rubber doll left in it. "Unless we want to play a game?"

The audience went wild, with only a few knowing the history behind the game. The packaging made it very clear this wasn't the audience or the place to play it in.

It hurt to laugh almost as much as it hurt me to suppress it, so I laughed and told him to put it away quickly. I didn't want more people to see than necessary.

"I'll go get your actual hospital bag," Travis said as he put the game back and zippered the bag.

"No, I don't want you leaving."

Jack offered next and then realized he didn't have his car. He came by ambulance.

"That's right. How did you get here, Travis? I hope you didn't drive!"

"Lucy drove my car actually. Thankfully, she was there and was level-minded. She even took pictures of the event. Tasteful ones, of course."

"I don't mind going to get your bag. It's time you have some time alone with your little one. If you don't mind me in your house, that is," Megan offered.

"Why don't we all drive with you. That way Jack can pick up his care and carry on with this day. Lucy can get hers and I'll take Travis's back, with the car seat and actual hospital bag."

Under the influence of medication and exhaustion, the whole thing confused me, but seemed to make sense to everyone else. I was starving for something other than hospital food so was getting impatient for someone to bring me something. And then Doctor Gee brought our little bundle of joy and my hunger pains dissipated.

Looking around the room at everyone before I was mostly alone, my heart swelled with knowing I finally had a family. It was a mixed up one and I wasn't sure Lucy would be considered, but our relationship seemed much more than a professional one.

The reports were all good ones and were given once the crowd left. They were all given clear instructions on visiting hours and limits of visitors so Jack and Lucy said their goodbyes and promises they would be back whenever I needed.

Travis stayed attentive and kind while clearly being hung over and tired himself. He slept in the chair beside me and I fell asleep watching him hold our little one so naturally. I woke to screams in what seemed like minutes though must have been at least an hour.

Startled so abruptly from my slumber, I was confused as to my surroundings when I awoke. I saw Travis first, trying to calm our baby by putting his pinky in her mouth. She suckled then quickly spit it out.

It was time for a decision - was I prepared to breast feed.

Travis handed her to me and mumbled sleepily that he was going to get a doctor.

It was the first time I was left alone with our baby girl. With any infant at all, for that matter.

It was scary as hell.

Chapter Forty-Three

Taking advantage of my brief moment of privacy and simply wanting our former angel to stop wailing, I folded down the top of my gown and tried to shove my nipple into her mouth. I wasn't patient, I wasn't experienced and, except for movies and intimate moments with Travis, my breasts were never really used before. She didn't latch as easily as I wanted her to and I was mortified.

When the door opened I quickly hid my breasts and sighed. "I guess it is formula for her." Thankfully it was a female nurse who appeared to be in her mid-fifties with Travis beside her. "Don't give up that easily, Mom. She's new at this, too. You need to relax and then she'll relax. Let's try again."

I tried to only expose one of my nipples, hoping the nurse didn't see while also knowing she had her own and would have seen many before. It was pointless, my trying to be discreet. The nurse, still anonymous, came over and began to massage my breast and work it into the tiny mouth.

"There, it just needed some relaxing and warming up. Your skin is mighty cold. I'll be back in a bit."

I loved watching and listening to her suckle as I filled my darling with nutrition though was frozen in place by the scene that just played out. Once the door was closed, Travis burst out in laughter. "Sorry, I couldn't hold it back any longer. That was weird!"

"And mortifying. I never thought I'd get the full treatment at a hospital!"

"It's beautiful though. Annabelle, you're beautiful."

I laughed in response while trying not to jiggle. My protégé was sound asleep sucking softly. "I'm hideous and disgusting. I need a shower and some food. I am starving."

"You are beautiful," he said again. "I'm sorry." He seemed to want to say a lot more but was interrupted by a doctor and team coming in.

"It's time for you to be moved, Annabelle. We're going to have one more look and check your numbers then move you into a ward."

Thankful the sleeper kept sleeping through the chaos, and just as thankful for the positive updates, I was dreading being moved. I was enjoying the big room and being alone, or mostly alone. "Is there a single room available?"

"We can certainly check, though I do know the ward you're going to is empty right now. Which would you prefer?"

"Oh, let's just go with the ward then," I muttered, seeing stress appear in Travis's face. He was so frugal despite our being just fine financially. Neither one of us could trust it long term so agreed it would be best to save and sacrifice where we could. Which was why being able to nurse offered so much relief. I hoped it could continue.

"Ok, Travis, time to go, can you gather her things? Annabelle, we'll get you a wheelchair." The team of professionals left as I tried to sit up.

"What things?" I didn't realize there was much more in the room than myself and our baby.

"Apparently Kate was back. The hospital bag is here along with some flowers and gifts. I didn't even know she came in."

"Me neither, but I'm glad she did. That granola bar please." I laid back down, not having much strength or balance to sit up on my own, especially while balancing a weight on my chest. She finally unlatched, stirred a little but seemed at peace. "Can you please cover me up?"

Travis came over and pulled up the gown, kissing our baby girl on the forehead as he did. Then giving me a kiss despite our terrible breaths.

"Travis, once I settle, why don't you go home and freshen up. There's not much for you to do here."

It took some convincing, but he finally went home. With our little one in her own bed and the room finally quiet, I had some peaceful sleep at last. Though it didn't last long as Jack appeared, along with Chris, the paramedic. They came in quietly but, being a first time mom, everything was waking me already. I looked at the bundle sleeping soundly and then to the men looking at her. They were adorable together, gazing at the little one resting peacefully.

We whispered and Jack asked if I was alright. I sensed he meant more than he said and knew he was referring to Travis being such a jerk. Assuring him I could take care of myself and would heal, he smiled and said he wanted to see me again once things settled.

He confessed he was going to be extra busy in the coming weeks with exams and work which would allow me time to get settled. "I apologize, though, I won't be able to attend any celebrations or really be around to help."

"Oh, geez. I wouldn't expect you to. We haven't seen each other in decades, there's no responsibility expected from you. I'll be fine."

"It doesn't feel like decades, although you have grown more confident and more beautiful in that time. Health wise, if you have any questions though, this man can help."

"Absolutely. I'm no expert but I know a few things. Having three younger siblings has taught me the practical and my studies have all the theories."

"That's so kind of you to offer. Hopefully I'll be sticking around here for a few days and then Travis took a month off of work so we should be OK. I appreciate it though."

"What's her name?" Chris asked as she stirred.

"Great question. We have it narrowed down but not confirmed yet. That will be our task once Travis returns."

She started crying softly and fussing. "May I?" Jack asked.

"Yes, of course."

Just as he picked her up Travis returned. Jack quickly handed her off to me and excused himself after giving me a look and my whispering that it was fine.

He left and Travis didn't say a word.

"Shall we name our little one?" I asked to relieve some tension as I maneuvered her to my breast.

Travis took a seat beside my bed and laid his hand on her head.

We looked at each other as we agreed on, "Abigail Terecia."

Chapter Forty-Four

After a few welcomed days in the hospital, I was ready to go home. I had enough of the poking and interruptions, the beeping and screaming from the delivery room. The doctor gave us the approval for the next day. I was grateful to have one more night in the hospital with the promise of going home in the morning.

Travis seemed more stressed when I told him the news. Thankfully, Megan and Kate were there to reassure him, promising him they were just a call away. Megan added, "And if she's anything like me at all, she'll be so much more comfortable and relaxed at home. Once you figure out your flow, all will be adjusted."

"Thanks, ladies. It will be easier with me not having to travel back and forth."

I sensed he wanted to add, 'and have control over the visitors,' so was impressed by his restraint. Everyone took a load of things home to make it easier for Travis the next day. It made the room feel empty until it wasn't.

My nights of having the big room to myself were over which made it even better that I would be moved out the next day. And it wasn't just mother and child, it appeared there was an exception made to visiting hours so father and three additional young kids were included. A package deal.

It made me thankful that Travis had already left and avoided the chaos. It also meant he avoided the uncomfortable way the man made me feel every time I breast fed. He was subtle about it but his glares were off putting. Despite the peep show I was giving to all of the medical professionals, and the increased level of comfort when Megan and Kate were in the room, I reached for my nursing blanket and covered up. Apparently the new mom wasn't a breast feeder or cut off all sexual adventures after the announcement of baby four. This man seemed deprived and creepy as heck.

It was going to be a long night, I thought.

And it was. After the man introduced himself and listed the names of his children and their mother he seemed to want to converse. I, on the other hand, wanted to read my book while Abi slept. I kept picking it up, hoping he would take the hint, though it seemed he simply wanted the escape from his own chaos.

It was the final straw when he tried to pick up Abi from her tiny crib. It didn't make any sense to me when he had his own little one to tend to. It made a fraction more sense when I realized he had all boys, including his newest, and all the boys were rowdy, but I wasn't comfortable with it at all and told him so. I was civil about it, with a hint of rude, and he flew off the handle which only worked to upset everyone in the room and some outside of the room.

A nurse came in to see what was happening. She looked at me, then at the family which wasn't easy as the three boys were running around and playing with medical equipment. "We'll need to ask you to leave. Visiting hours are over," she announced. When the man and kids didn't make an effort to go, the nurse followed up with, "I mean you. I'll need to call security if you don't leave now."

The man looked mortified. It appeared that he was used to being in charge and not ordered around. It was the mother who finally spoke up in apology and said, "They will be gone in ten minutes."

"Make it five," the nurse ordered as she came to my bedside. "Are you ok? I know this isn't ideal. This was done because you only have one night to go. Putting them in the other rooms would have made them too crowded."

"It's fine. Just please, close my curtains. Thank you for making them leave."

She left the room after closing my curtains and returning in three minutes, checking that the family left and, by the sounds of it, cleaning up what the young boys disturbed. I asked her for assistance and asked if she could open my curtains again. I felt it rude to be shut off from the only other occupant in the room, even under these circumstances.

When the curtains were pulled back I sat up to see the woman feeding her newborn with formula. It looked so much easier, the baby took to it right away and drank it all. I was jealous until I realized how much I was finally enjoying nursing. And knew I'd lose the pregnancy wait much faster this way.

Holding Abi close to me, watching her tiny eye lids close or her bright pupils look around. Easy wasn't necessarily better when it came to parenting and I knew I had a lot to learn. Each decision, as with life in general, had its pros and cons though I was thankful I pushed through. It was also in that moment that I decided not to hide under a blanket.

I wouldn't be posting selfies on social media any time soon though if it was time for baby to eat, no matter where I was, I would try not to be embarrassed.

Looking over to the windowsill, I saw that Travis left the laptop and was grateful. I had a blog to write and an announcement of my impending absence. Carefully getting out of the bed, just as much for Abi's sake as my own frailty, I laid her gently in her bed and hobbled over to the laptop.

I jumped when the lady finally spoke, "Do I know you?"

I turned to her as I made my way back to bed. She didn't look familiar at all. "I don't think so. I'm Annabelle. Congratulations on your growing family! You must have your hands full at home."

"Yes, yes! Annabelle. I do know you, though you don't know me. Why would you? I'm a stay at home mom. The only peace I get is when I am in the bathroom and it's there I read your blog! It keeps me sane like nothing else!"

Being in the public eye wasn't something I was used to yet. I knew posting my picture with the blog was the personal thing to do, it helped put a face to a name, it just made it weird when someone recognized me before I even met them. Considering myself an introvert, I opened up behind the computer not realizing I'd be opening myself up so much outside the screen.

"Thank you. Yes, you're right, I'm Annabelle. I'm always so shocked to find a fan. I just started this as a hobby, to think people are actually reading it is mind-blowing."

"My husband has actually been sending you emails. Lots of them. Now we understand why they have gone unanswered. Maybe you can reply now, since you have your laptop?"

Chapter Forty-Five

I was speechless. Did I read her husband's emails and send them to spam? Why would he be writing me?

I didn't answer. Just made my way back into the bed, covered myself with the thin sheet and opened my laptop. The woman from across the room continued to stare, clearly expecting an answer.

"I'll check. What's his name again?"

As she spelled his name I typed it in the search bar, trying to type with crossed fingers. Hoping that my computer wouldn't connect, that the power would go out, that someone would interrupt us and distract her. None of that happened so I announced that I found them.

Scrolling back to the first one received I noticed the address. He worked at a publishing company. Apparently, the man I just felt accosted by was a literary agent seeking to work with me on publishing a book. I cringed, not imagining myself working for someone like him. In a way he reminded me of Chuck and I vowed to never work for a man like him again.

And then it hit me – a book! Someone wanted to help me publish a book.

I kept reading through the emails with very mixed emotions, trying hard to refrain from reacting externally. By the end of the email chain I was as equally thrilled by the proposition as I was disgusted by who was sending it. Then I hoped I was wrong, that the first impression was exaggerated and he really wasn't that bad of a man. Maybe I could work with him.

I took more time reading through them again, trying to formulate a response as I skimmed over the text. When I finally found a way to speak, I looked over to see the woman sound asleep and let out a sigh of relief.

My response could wait.

I emailed Travis instead. Forwarding one of the emails that clarified the great potential and offer. I added a note at the top explaining that my room was no longer my own and I was eager to see him in the morning.

Not waiting for a reply, I quietly closed the laptop, struggled to put it on the table beside me and fell asleep quickly with a smile on my face.

Waking way too early for my liking to the sound of toddlers fighting, it took a minute before I recalled what I read last night. I thought it was a dream at first then I saw the nightmare. Hoping that I could stay off the radar while they handled family stuff, I escaped to the washrooms and fed Abi. Thankfully the room had two washrooms so I didn't feel rushed. Staying in there until it quieted down, I dressed awkwardly while holding Abi still and then laying her on the floor for just a moment, protected, of course, with my hospital gown.

Grateful Travis packed my comfy pants, they still went on snuggly. I remembered the doctors and nurses saying it could take a few weeks for my belly to contract. I wasn't sure I would be comfortable waiting at least the three months before joining the gym again, as advised. Then again, maybe I wouldn't even bother going back.

Getting terribly bored in the bathroom, I came out immediately when I heard Travis's voice. Hugging him, carefully with Abi between us, I whispered to him that we needed to leave quickly. Unfortunately, he didn't understand why and quickly, plus loudly, congratulated me on my potential book offer. I cringed, and he rushed to get me the wheelchair that appeared in the room. "Are you ok?" He said this at the same time the man approached us. Thinking quickly, on my feet or rather on my ass, I pretended to faint. I hoped I could explain my actions to Travis and have him understand once we were outside of the hospital.

I heard him call for a nurse in an urgent voice as he bent down and checked my pulse. It seemed an odd thing for him to do, but we all act so strangely under stress. Poor guy.

Several nurses came, surrounded me and the nurse from the previous night closed the curtains as they looked me over. Once it sounded like the curtains were closed and the man excused I opened my eyes and whispered that I was fine. "I simply need to avoid that man. I'm ready to get home. I'll explain later, Travis. Please, take me home." I looked him in the eyes and tried to apologize more with my look. I knew he was upset and hurt that I went to such an extent and had him so worried.

My favourite nurse decided on a plan and advised us of the details. Travis would stay behind, they would rush me out, saying they needed to do testing and eventually return, without me, to let Travis know I had to be moved to another room and to gather my things.

With the plan in motion, I stepped into the role of ailing patient and Travis into concerned partner. I took a peek to see him strapping Abigail into the car seat and motioning for a nurse to check it. When I left he was twiddling his thumbs, an act he only did once in front of me and it was about eight months prior at our first appointment. He was stressed.

Closing my eyes again and being pushed out, the motion almost made me actually sick but then it stopped. I was given the all clear once I was down the hall and around the corner. One nurse said she would send Travis down in a few minutes and I was all set to leave. Her words made me feel better than I had in a long time.

It seemed like a very long and boring wait but finally Travis and Abigail appeared. I told him again that I was sorry and asked if he would take me home. "Are you able to walk or can you take Abigail with the car seat?"

Thankfully a nurse overheard us and advised that it was policy for a new mom to be wheeled out.

"I'll get someone, as they need to check the car seat in your vehicle anyway."

The waiting was rough, especially with the possibility of the man coming around the corner any second. Thankfully, someone came before he was seen and escorted us out. Giving Travis the all clear once she verified he had Abigail in correctly.

On the ride home I explained why I did what I did. Travis wasn't thrilled but said he understood and was grateful to have me home again.

As we turned the corner to our street I saw the driveway filled with cars and balloons flying from our mailbox.

"Travis, what is happening?"

Chapter Forty-Six

It should have been a dumb question though I needed to ask it. Never before has someone thrown me a party or celebration of any sort. Even at work, despite all other employees getting cupcakes for their anniversary and birthday, I remained invisible. It was usually easier that way though it always hurt.

This was a new feeling. One I wasn't used to. I burst into tears and blamed it on the hormones once Travis asked. He pulled in, parked the car and asked if I was ready.

"I guess so, I'm not sure what to prepare for really."

"Then let's go." He was excited, seeming to forget that he was mad at me just moments before, and he rushed to open my door than get Abigail.

"Did you do all of this?"

"I had no part in it. The girls hated that they didn't have your baby shower in time so improvised. I knew it was happening but was sworn to secrecy."

He somehow managed to balance the car seat on his arm, hold my and open the door. Our house was filled with people, decorations and food. I looked to Travis then to Abi, who was somehow sleeping through all the commotion, and then back to the friends who gathered to welcome us home.

I was speechless, especially when I saw *my* Jack. I never imagined that Travis would let him into our home.

Jack rushed over and offered to get Abigail to her crib. Travis conceded and handed her over then helped me to the new lazy boy by the big living room window. "This was my idea. You need a place to be comfortable and rock. I also have a rocking chair for the nursery being delivered tomorrow."

"Oh, it's perfect, Travis." I sat down and felt enveloped by comfort.

Over the next hour I was served many delightfully delicious plates of a wide variety of foods, complete with conversation and drinks. When my bladder couldn't hold anymore, I had Travis help me to the washroom where I changed my hospital provided pad. They were thick and uncomfortable but absolutely necessary, especially on the new furniture. I was warned that it could be awhile before I could stop wetting myself and Kegel exercises were highly encouraged. I had no idea what the doctor was talking about and Travis assured me he would explain, gladly.

I tried doing a few while Travis waited though failed miserably. Guests were waiting and my nipples began leaking so I knew to expect Abigail to be hungry soon. As I flushed the toilet and pulled up my pants I heard her start to cry.

Travis guided me back to the living room and rushed to get Abigail, bringing her to me. "Oh, did you want some privacy?"

"Nah, we're all family here," I said as I bravely unfolded my maternity bra and attempted to feed my newborn. I tried to look more confident than I was, especially when she didn't latch right away and when I saw Jack approach I was mortified. "Let me help," he offered. Travis lost all colour in his face as he watched another man bend down and touch his girlfriend's breast, positioning it easily into Abigail's mouth.

When he stood and noticed Travis's fists were clenched he apologized and then said, "Travis, before you hit me, let me introduce you to someone. Chris, come here please." I noticed for the first time that the knitting paramedic was in attendance. "Travis and Annabelle, now that we're together under calmer circumstances, let me introduce you to my boyfriend."

"You're gay?" Travis yelled.

"Well, yes, I guess this makes me gay or, in more acceptable terms, a homosexual. This was what I told Annabelle at supper. I never got the chance to tell you before. I realize it may come as a surprise, but I was not trying to steal your girlfriend. That's not the type of man I am."

"I wanted to tell you, Travis but it was not my place. And circumstances didn't allow."

"What a relief!" Travis sighed in delight. "What an idiot I was. I'm sorry, Annabelle, and Jack.

Pregnancy hormones had me acting stupid, apparently."

"You're forgiven only if you'll allow me to be a part of your lives."

"Yes, of course. Please."

In that awkward moment I, for the first time, noticed what was playing on the television. A loop of a selection of my photo shoot with Tara was running and I had to laugh through my embarrassment. The photos were gorgeous, even if they were of me and some of Travis and me. Then it got to a selection of the shots when the dog came in and some were absolutely hilarious. What really tickled me was the fact that Travis had an erection the entire time. I called him over while trying not to cause a scene. "Travis, did you see these?"

"Not yet but I gave my permission to show them. I hope you don't mind. These are just a tasteful few. She promised to hold back the more promiscuous ones for a private viewing."

I admired his bravery and took his hand, urging him to bend down so I could whisper, "Check out your erection." He instinctively looked down, assuming I was referring to now but then realized I meant the photos. He squeezed my hand and whispered back, "Always, baby." I noticed he was getting a little excited and may have been the reason he excused himself and went back to the conversation with Jack.

As they chatted and others ate, and swooned over the new mom and her baby, I took a moment to check my phone. Emails were piling up again and I just scrolled through the subject lines quickly as I fed Abigail.

One in particular caught my eye. A big five publisher had emailed me last week with an offer. A legitimate offer to publish my blogs in book format, as long as I would include some new content that wasn't yet public. The advance being suggested was substantial and the contract seemed straight-forward.

I put the phone down and looked at my sweet girl looking back up at me. Then I looked around the room, noting Jack and Travis talking like old friends, Megan and Kate chatting like sisters, and others buzzing around making sure the place was kept tidy and putting meals into the freezer that I could easily make later. Tara was in the background taking pictures of the entire party for which I was thankful. I knew I wouldn't remember everything that was happening that day but there was one thing I knew for certain.

For as much as lost when I turned forty, I gained so much more, including weight, at forty-one. And I could only wonder what year forty-two would hold.

Gratitude and Acknowledgements

While this story is fictitious, many people inspired it and I would be remiss to not include some of them.

First, my husband, always. IIis belief in my passion is phenomenal. He has pushed, pleaded and prodded at all the right times and in all the right places to encourage my writing endeavours. Without him, there would be no romance.

And my son for his love of reading, giving me hope that the next generation will love books as much as I do.

For Edie, for being my "easy" friend and celebrating the "easy" parts of me.

Scott, at Newhook Designs; you are outstanding. Your creative genius, thrive for knowledge and ability to meet deadlines is phenomenal. Thank you.

Tracy Nickerson, a woman I haven't yet met in person though has always been that embrace when I needed it more. She is always my first beta reader and always, always has kind and constructive feedback for me, not to mention begs for more.

For Jenn Carson who simply said one night, "Just write." I don't think she had any idea what that those two little words would turn into.

For Tara who answered the question of what would be next for Annie. While many were asking for a sequel, her casually mentioned idea sparked so much and answered at least one thing for me. And yes, she is a boudoir photographer who has a dog and no, I haven't had her shoot me… yet….

And for all of you, dear readers, for without you my imagination captured would never grow wings.

Please, if you have a moment to spare, leave an honest review where ever books are sold.

And check out my other books.

www.ingramcontent.com/pod-product-compliance
Lightning Source LLC
Chambersburg PA
CBHW071821020726
47502CB00004B/1195